Scandal Could Ruin
Her Political Career.

Wallis surprised herself—not only for accepting Sam's dinner invitation, but for inviting him to spend the night.

"Are you sure about this?" he asked.

"Of course I am," she said softly, pulling his face near hers. "But what about you?"

"It's different for me," he said. "I won't have to get up and run a city council meeting tomorrow."

"I make an effort to keep politics out of the bedroom." Wallis smiled.

"It seems to me that we're wasting a perfectly good bed, Your Honor," Sam said as he reached for the edge of her shirt and pulled it over her head.

SUZANNE MICHELLE

can't decide which she loves more—her family or writing. She lives in Texas and often writes about the West, which she knows so well. When she's not busy writing she's often to be found with her nose in a book, because reading is another one of her favorite activities.

Dear Reader:

SILHOUETTE DESIRE is an exciting new line of contemporary romances from Silhouette Books. During the past year, many Silhouette readers have written in telling us what other types of stories they'd like to read from Silhouette, and we've kept these comments and suggestions in mind in developing SILHOUETTE DESIRE.

DESIREs feature all of the elements you like to see in a romance, plus a more sensual, provocative story. So if you want to experience all the excitement, passion and joy of falling in love, then SILHOUETTE DESIRE is for you.

Karen Solem
Editor-in-Chief
Silhouette Books

SUZANNE MICHELLE
Political Passions

Silhouette Desire
Published by Silhouette Books New York
America's Publisher of Contemporary Romance

SILHOUETTE BOOKS, a Division of Simon & Schuster, Inc.
1230 Avenue of the Americas, New York, N.Y. 10020

Copyright © 1984 by Suzanne Michelle

Distributed by Pocket Books

ISBN: 0-671-47116-3

First Silhouette Books printing April, 1984

10 9 8 7 6 5 4 3 2 1

America's Publisher of Contemporary Romance

Printed in the U.S.A.

BC91

Books by Suzanne Michelle

Silhouette Desire

Enchanted Desert #29
Silver Promises #47
No Place for a Woman #57
Stormy Serenade #76
Recipe for Love #87
Fancy Free #106
Political Passions #128

Political
Passions

1

The beautifully restored rooms of the Cotton Exchange building were filled with soft music. People clad in every variety of elegant evening dress danced or simply sipped champagne, and the eyes of the crowd were securely focused on one woman whose natural beauty and poise were enhanced by her long white silk dress, its elegant length gracefully sweeping the dance floor as she turned and swirled, easily following her partner's lead.

And that's me, Wallis Carmichael thought with a chuckle of delighted glee. Her face was calm and composed, as befitted the newly inaugurated mayor of one of the nation's largest cities, but beneath her poise she felt a thrill of pleasure she had never known before. Nothing, not even election night, could compare to this day, the day on which she took up the reins of government. She dutifully followed her partner's intricate dance steps, smiling up at him with an expression of pure pleasure as they executed a difficult turn.

"I'm so proud of you, honey," the man said, a twinkle in his deep brown eyes.

The amber eyes turned up to him were as intelligent as they were lovely. Wallis tossed a stray strand of chestnut hair back over her shoulder with a slender, graceful hand. "Thanks, Dad," she returned, her glance filled with daughterly affection. "But I couldn't have done it without you."

"Oh, hush," he said in a low voice. "You're going to be the best mayor this city has ever seen. I know it."

"I'm going to try," she promised firmly. "I want to make you proud of me."

"I'm already proud of you, honey. I was proud when you went to Harvard Law School, I was proud when you served on the city council, and I see no reason not to be proud of you now that you're the mayor. You're still my daughter. And I respect your political ambitions and achievements, though I wonder sometimes if you haven't paid too high a price for them." He looked down at her questioningly.

Wallis answered him with quiet dignity. "I haven't. This is what I want—what I've always wanted. I've never been so happy."

"That's what I wanted to hear," he said, laughing. "As long as you're happy, I'm happy. Now I'm afraid

I'm going to have to leave. I see your mother over there waving. We're off to the ranch tomorrow. Call if you need anything."

"I will," Wallis promised. "Don't think about me—just enjoy yourselves." The music stopped and the two of them stood there for a moment, Judge Carmichael bending down to give his daughter a paternal peck on the cheek. The reporters swooped down on them to capture the moment, lights flashing everywhere. Wallis gave her father's hand a final squeeze and waved to her mother as she turned to face them.

I might as well get used to this, she told herself resolutely. It goes with the territory. She knew she looked lovely, the long dress skimming the feminine contours of her slender frame, the simple scoop neck revealing the softness of her breasts. Her long chestnut hair framed her face like a velvet curtain, the red highlights gleaming in the light. The porcelain whiteness of her skin was smooth as silk and had a clean, scrubbed freshness that glowed with the barest touch of makeup. She radiated poise and authority, and the reporters gathered around her seemed to sense it. She noticed that they waited respectfully for her to complete each answer before asking the next question.

Their questions were not difficult ones, but Wallis was grateful when her chief administrative aide and campaign manager, Ivy Tucker, appeared at her side and gave the press the high sign. "Don't you think you've had enough, guys? This is supposed to be a celebration, remember?" The gorgeous blonde jokingly freed Wallis from their clutches and led her over to a buffet table, handing her a glass of champagne.

"Thanks," Wallis said appreciatively, "but that wasn't so bad, most of them are really nice."

"Tonight, yes—they are nice," Ivy agreed. "But mark my words, tomorrow the honeymoon's over. They'll be dogging your every step. Do you have any idea how many requests I've had from reporters who want to trail you around on your first full day in office?"

"Oh, no," Wallis groaned. "What did you tell them?"

"Easy." Ivy grinned. "I told them your office wouldn't hold them all and had them draw straws, so only two of them will be shadowing you all day, though I don't doubt that the others will pop up at every opportunity."

"No problem." Wallis laughed, admiring her aide's solution. "I can live with two shadows. It's only for a day."

"That's the spirit," Ivy agreed. "It never hurts to keep the press happy. And you're hot copy right now. You wouldn't believe all the requests from television talk shows on my desk already."

Wallis grimaced. "Those you can turn down. Where were all those people during the campaign when I wanted to talk about issues?"

"Well, you won, didn't you?" Ivy teased her. "Now you can talk about issues. Now you're the boss."

Wallis grinned, infected by Ivy's good humor. She turned as she felt a tap on her shoulder and looked up to see the florid face of Ernie Dayton, newly reelected to the city council.

"Hello, little lady," he boomed, and Wallis flinched at the sound. Ernie was going to be a problem, she had known that, but she hadn't expected him to start in on her so soon.

"Good evening, Mr. Dayton," she returned coolly. "Enjoying yourself?" She was determined to get along with this man, but it wasn't going to be easy. Dayton had a lot of power—he'd been on the city council for as long as she could remember, and they'd tangled on many an issue. A wealthy conservative from one of the older, more affluent sections of Houston, he had always been suspect in her mind, but she had never been able to find out anything underhanded about him. Nevertheless, she sometimes wondered if he really had the best interests of the city at heart.

"Oh, it's a lovely party," he boomed, his face turning even redder. "The missus and I have been to so many of these inaugural celebrations, you know. But this one is certainly different."

Wallis knew he was referring to its size and location and decided it simply wasn't worth the effort to confront him. "I had hoped it would be," she said pleasantly. "I didn't see any sense in paying a fortune for a huge gathering at a hotel, when a smaller celebration is just as appropriate—and certainly less expensive. And the Cotton Exchange is one of our historic landmarks—what could be more perfect?"

"I'm sure you have a point," he blustered. "You always do. But I'm also sure that most of the city would have preferred a grander celebration. Have to keep up the image, you know."

Wallis's answering smile was a little stiff. "Mr. Dayton, I might remind you that one of my campaign promises was to save the city money. Starting now. Tonight. I try to keep my promises."

Ernie's red face seemed just about to explode when he and Wallis were interrupted by a cool, urbane voice behind them. "Hardly a quorum for a city council meeting," the voice said drily. Wallis greeted the speaker, a longtime friend and another newly reelected member of the city council, Graham Davis, with a smile of relief.

"Oh, Graham, I'm so glad to see you," she said, and the words were heartfelt. She had known the attractive older man for years and had always respected him as a person as well as a politician. She had worked well with him in the past and was looking forward to doing so again in the future.

"You really shouldn't be grinding political axes at a time like this, Ernie," Graham said with a distasteful glance in the other man's direction. "It's just not proper. This is a celebration, and a lovely one at that. Shall we dance, Wallis?"

"Delighted," she agreed, and they danced away, leaving an exasperated Ernie Dayton staring after them.

"Was he giving you a hard time?" Graham asked. "I don't mean to pry, but . . ."

"Not really," Wallis asserted proudly. "It seems that he would have preferred a gaudier celebration, that's about the size of it. Nothing I couldn't handle."

"I'm sure of it," Graham said smoothly, as he gracefully led her in a waltz. Wallis glanced up at the silver-haired man with gratitude, knowing that he wouldn't press her. "He's just a good ol' boy. You've got to remember that everything you stand for irritates him. You should know that from working with him—or trying to—on the city council. It offends him that the mayor is a woman, and a pretty one at that. You do look fantastic this evening, you know. Just the way a newly elected, inaugurated mayor ought to look. And your father certainly seems proud."

Wallis smiled at the reference to her father, who was one of Graham's oldest friends. "He is. And that makes me happy. Happier."

"Enjoy it now," Graham cautioned. "Life's going to get a lot tougher faster than you think. Not that you're not up to the job. I know you are. I just wish you had something—or someone—special in your life besides politics. I worry about that."

"You and my father!" Wallis teased. "What is it about you two? Here I am, mayor of one of the largest cities in the country, and all you two can think about is marrying me off. I can't think of a single man who'd have me. I love my work too much. There's no room for anything else."

Graham smiled, acknowledging her reproof. "Still and all, it seems a shame."

"Now stop that," Wallis insisted. "When the right man comes along, I'll know it. Just give me time."

"Right," Graham kidded. "You want us to give you the one thing you don't have—time. You dedicated career politicians."

The music was coming to an end. "You're a fine one to talk," Wallis said teasingly as she headed toward Ivy, who was beckoning to her.

Ivy was talking to a few of the major contributors to Wallis's campaign, and Wallis spent the obligatory few minutes thanking them for their support. It wasn't something she minded at all, for she did appreciate the people who had made her campaign possible and successful. She was a perfect politician, born and bred. She knew all the rules. But still, there was something different about her—an air of true concern, of genuine human interest, that set her apart from the others. She was in politics for all the right reasons, and she knew it.

Somehow other people sensed this about her, which was why she'd been so successful at such an early age. Of course, being a beautiful young woman from one of the city's oldest families didn't hurt, but Wallis never traded on her looks or her background. Her greatest strength lay in what she was—a good person who really cared.

"I'm a little tired, Ivy," she whispered as the political well-wishers walked away. "I know this is my special night, but it has been a long day."

"You can't leave yet," Ivy insisted. "Take a break. Have a drink, go to the ladies' room or something. It just wouldn't do to leave so soon."

"All right," Wallis agreed, trusting her aide's good instincts. "I'll just go out for a breath of fresh air and then I'll be right back."

Oh, for a cigarette, she thought to herself, as she went toward the door. If her mother could hear that, she'd die. Wallis smiled, remembering her mother's countless admonitions that no lady ever smoked in public. And of course, Wallis never did. But at the moment, she longed for the release of tension, the soothing ritual of a cigarette.

When she got to the door, she saw a uniformed policeman holding back a crowd of reporters, all of whom shouted at each other when they caught a glimpse of her. Wallis smiled at them and continued walking down the hallway. Not again, she thought, not now. If I could just have a few minutes to myself, I could come back and give them all the answers they want. She looked about for a means of escape, and her eyes saw the door marked STAIRS just as she remembered that it should be there somewhere. Ducking gratefully into the stairwell, she began to climb, enjoying the stretching, demanding exercise after the long hours of dancing and standing around. She climbed to the top and tried the door that led to the roof. It was unlocked.

Cool January air greeted Wallis as she threw the door open. She shivered a bit in the thin silk dress, but the cold was bracing and energizing. She walked out onto the roof and went over to the side facing Main Street, looking down at the lights of the bright thoroughfare.

She had grown up here, had spent her entire life in this city except for the three years she had been at Harvard, and even then she had found her thoughts constantly returning to the city on the bayou. When she was elected to the city council after a long and arduous campaign, she had been exhilarated, thinking that now she could give back something to the city that had given her and her family such joy.

Oh, the place had problems, all right, and serious ones—the growing pains of a boomtown that had gotten too big too fast. But Wallis was prepared to tackle those problems, to find the answers to such diverse plagues as pollution, a snarled traffic system, and inefficient mass transit. The list went on and on. But like the city, she was young and full of energy, and she knew she could at least help to make life better there, even if she couldn't make the problems disappear. She was intelligent, well educated, and determined.

"I love this city," she said again, aloud this time.

"And from all practical appearances, it loves you back," came a low male voice at her elbow.

Wallis jumped, startled by the unexpected sound, and her eyes scanned the darkness, searching for the face of the intruder. "I beg your pardon?" she inquired, a little taken aback at being observed in a rare private moment.

"Well, if the crowd downstairs and the crowd

outside are any indication, you're certainly going to be the most popular mayor this city has ever had." The voice was caressing, soothing, and very, very masculine.

"Thank you," Wallis responded with her usual honesty. No sense in pretending false modesty. She stood silently, waiting for his next move, wondering who this man was.

The sudden flare of a cigarette lighter illuminated his strong features. He had sharp, intelligent eyes— even in the dark, she could tell they were blue—a straight nose, and a mouth that curved with sensuality. His blond hair shone in the brief light, then darkness was between them again. "Care for a cigarette?" came the voice.

"I really shouldn't," Wallis said longingly. She had to laugh, remembering what she had been thinking only a few moments before. "My mother always told me a true lady never smokes in public, and I try not to."

"You succeed," he answered. "I don't think that there's a single mention of your smoking in any of the articles about you. But go ahead, take one. I'll never tell."

Something about his tone of voice dared her to do it. "Why, thank you, I will," she said, calmly accepting the case he pulled out of a pocket of his evening jacket, while he reached for the lighter with his other hand. She took out a cigarette, absently placing the case in the pocket of her evening dress. She bent forward to the light, noticing his strong hand, with its long, tapering fingers curving around the lighter. Instinctively she reached out to place her hand on his and their fingers met in electric contact. Wallis drew back, inhaling deeply, while in reality trying to recover from the shock of the brief touch. She was moved, remembering romantic scenes from the movies she loved so much, thinking about all the heroes who had lit cigarettes for beautiful women. Damn, that's where I ought to be, she thought. Curled up at home with my video cassette player and a bowl of popcorn, watching Spencer Tracy or Humphrey Bogart. Not here on some rooftop with a stranger.

"Thank you," she said, walking over to the edge and leaning against the low barrier that ran around the building. He followed her—she could feel it, just as she could hear his soft footsteps behind her. She was momentarily afraid—not that he would harm her—but she was afraid of herself, of the emotions that raced through her at the touch of her hand on his.

Oh, Wallis, you've been watching too many old movies, she admonished herself, waiting for him to speak.

"It's a beautiful night for an inaugural ball," he said softly, his voice close to her ear. The words, which might have seemed trite or predictable coming from someone else, seemed entirely appropriate for the moment.

She laughed with pleasure, wanting him to share it with her. "If you ask me, any night would have been lovely. Even if it had been raining cats and dogs—even if we'd been in the middle of a hurricane, though it's hardly the season for it. This is the most special night of my life. It's what I've always wanted, wished for, dreamed of." She stopped, wondering what it was about this man that inspired her to speak this way, for she was usually an emotionally reticent person, not given to sharing intimate feelings.

"Be careful what you wish for . . ." the voice began.

"I know," Wallis laughed. "I might get it. Well, I wished for it, and I've got it, and I still wish for it. I'm going to make this an even more wonderful city to live in. No matter what it takes."

"Now that is the voice of a determined woman," he commented softly, tossing his cigarette to the cement and taking a brief step to put it out. Wallis inhaled once more, then followed suit.

"I *am* determined." She said with pride.

"A kiss for luck then," he said, leaning forward. Wallis didn't have a moment to resist before she was in his arms. He was taller than she had realized, and his arms went around her in a powerful embrace, drawing her body, shivering under the thin silk of the dress, next to his own strong form. His lips found hers surely and swiftly, and what began as a gentle kiss sparked into a mutual flame of desire.

Wallis surrendered to the spell of the evening, the lights of the city, the sweet taste of success, and more than that, the feeling of being desired—passionately desired—by the man who was holding her so firmly in his arms. As her lips parted beneath his, she felt a momentary urge to break the spell, to withdraw. This was not what she should be doing. But it was what she wanted to be doing, and she always took what she wanted from each moment, as much as she could. There would be precious little time for love in the days ahead. She deserved a little tonight.

When the kiss ended, he drew back and looked down at her, his expression unreadable because of the darkness. Wallis stood apart from him, shivering in the night air without the protection of his warm body against hers. "Good luck," he said softly. "Not that I think you'll need it."

Wallis smiled as his words caressed her as surely as his lips had only moments before. She leaned forward, her hand searching out his face in the darkness, stroking the strong line of his jaw. "I believe you mean that," she breathed softly.

"Oh, I do. More than you can know." Then he turned on his heel and walked away. The brief light from the opening door lit up his tall lean figure for a moment, then darkness descended again as the door closed behind him. Wallis failed to recognize him in that fleeting instant. Her hand closed around the metal of the cigarette case in her pocket and she instinctively started after him. But the moment, what had been shared between them, was over.

Wallis stood there for a few moments, savoring the

night air and the sudden chill, remembering the warmth of that all-too-brief kiss, and knowing some-how that she could trust the man's discretion—could probably trust him with anything. But she wondered who he was, and when, or if, she would ever find out.

2

Wallis stood looking out of the large plate glass window in her office, her tall, slender profile outlined by the brilliant blue of the day outside. Her tweed suit was the same chestnut color as her hair, and the amber silk shirt that matched her eyes was accented with a black silk bow tie. Her intelligent gaze was fixed on the city below, teeming with cars and people. The downtown streets were crowded even in the middle of the day. At five o'clock, the traffic would be bumper to bumper.

Wallis had just come out of her first city council meeting as mayor, where she had placed the name of Patten Roberts in nomination for the new director of the mass transit system. By and large, she was satisfied with the way things had progressed, though her political acumen told her that this appointment would not be made without a battle. Her experience as a council member stood her in good stead—she had had no difficulty running the meeting smoothly and efficiently, in spite of the almost immediate rumblings from Ernie Dayton and Ellie Johnson, both of whom could be counted on to express the conservative voice of the Old Guard. Wallis had not been surprised at their ill-disguised hostility, and she knew that this opposition had little to do with Patten Roberts himself but was rather an indication of the resistance to change of any sort. Somehow, she would have to win over this conservative group if she were going to accomplish anything at all.

Lost in thought, Wallis thrust her hands in the pockets of her suit jacket, and when her fingers touched the silver cigarette case in her pocket, its smooth surface interrupted only by the rough texture of engraved initials—S. D.—her attention was momentarily diverted. Her mind turned to the mysterious stranger she had met three days ago. Met? she asked herself ruefully. That's hardly the word for it. She didn't even know who he was. The only clue she had was the cigarette case in her pocket, and that wasn't much of a clue. It was sterling silver—an expensive cigarette case, maybe a gift, but undoubtedly valuable. She looked at the initials again, half hoping she would see something more. Maybe she should check the guest list for the inaugural ball.

Oh, don't be silly, she admonished herself, turning from the window to her desk. She had a thousand and one things to do that day. She certainly didn't have time to go through the guest list looking for the name that matched the initials. Wallis took the case out of her pocket. Like the glass slipper, she mused, it's all I've got. And for a moment, she fancied the notion of searching the kingdom for its owner. An amusing thought, she laughed to herself, as she mentally compared Prince Charming's kingdom to this sprawling city.

Turning the silver case over in her hand, Wallis sat down at her desk. She found herself recalling the sensuous details of that kiss on the rooftop: the rough texture of his hands as they encircled her waist, the tenderness of his lips on hers, the erotic rush that swept through her body. It was not a kiss she would soon forget, and yet . . . there was nothing she could put her finger on, nothing concrete to explain the special quality of that moment, no way to explain how quickly and easily she had opened up to this man in the night.

Enough of this, she said to herself as she slipped the case back in the pocket of her suit jacket. She was far too disciplined to allow herself more than a few moments of romantic daydreaming. And she certainly had no intention of brooding over the past—the future held too much for her. This was an expensive cigarette case. If it was at all important to this man, *he* would call *her*. He would certainly know where to find her. With that thought, she resolutely turned her attention to the list on her desk of things to be done that afternoon.

Just as she was about to call Ivy, the door opened and the cheerful aide bustled in with a tray of sandwiches and coffee and a steno pad under her arm. Ivy worried constantly that Wallis didn't eat properly, and she was ever on the alert for a chance to upgrade her diet. Wallis didn't object to Ivy's motherly concern. On the contrary, she was grateful for the gentle reminders from this woman who had been at her side since the beginning of her mayoral campaign. Though Wallis was careful to schedule some personal time in every day, it was all too easy to forget about food.

"Soup's on." Ivy's cheerful greeting brought Wallis back to the present.

"Mmmm. That coffee smells wonderful. And sandwiches, too." Wallis got up and met Ivy halfway. She took the tray from her and carried it to the desk.

"This is the only free lunch time you have this week. I knew if I didn't send out for something, you'd forget to eat." Ivy sat down in the chair across the desk from Wallis and opened her note pad.

"You think of everything," Wallis said with a grin. She hungrily bit into one of the sandwiches while she poured a cup of coffee for Ivy.

"That's what I'm paid to do," Ivy said matter-of-factly, taking the mug from Wallis. Her tone of voice signaled the end of the amenities. It was obvious that her thoughts were already returning to the business at hand. "Mr. Davis called for an appointment. Says he needs to see you this afternoon if possible."

Wallis sat down at her desk and took a sip of coffee. "I bet he wants to talk about Patten Roberts," she mused, shrewdly sizing up the situation. "Sure, I'll see him. Is there any time available this afternoon?"

"Well, you have an appointment with Chief Johnson at one, and at two o'clock with the committee from the chamber of commerce. That's it until three-thirty when you have to be at the zoo."

"Oh, that is today, isn't it?" Wallis looked down at the list on her desk again. "I had forgotten all about the pandas."

"I'm afraid I haven't been able to forget about them," Ivy said ruefully. "Mr. Tsien, the Chinese ambassador, called twice yesterday and again this morning. He was a little concerned about the facilities at the zoo, but I assured him that every care is being taken. I think he felt better when I told him a special suite of air-conditioned rooms is being built just for the pandas. I think his main worry was our hot Texas summers."

"Well, it sounds as if you told him all the right things. You do that so well, Ivy. I don't know what I'd do without you." Wallis's thanks came straight from the heart. Managing this office was no small task, and yet her assistant made it seem easy as pie. Ivy was always the first there in the morning and the last to leave at night.

Wallis flashed a smile at Ivy, but already her mind had returned to Graham Davis. "Tell Graham I'll be able to see him for a few minutes about two forty-five. That should give me enough time to be at the zoo by three-thirty." Even as she talked, she was mentally clocking the distance from City Hall to Hermann Park.

"I'll call him and let him know, then I'll be going out to the zoo about three to be sure everything is in order," Ivy said. "It's not every day the People's Republic of China gives us a pair of pandas. This is no time for us to drop the ball. Besides," Ivy explained with a little smile, "I'm looking forward to seeing the pandas myself."

"I know what you mean," Wallis agreed. "I've only read about them in books. They're going to be a good addition to the zoo. I assume the press will be there?"

"Oh, my goodness, yes. Though they're going to be more interested in you than in the pandas. We won't be able to control the reporters at a public place like the zoo, so we'd better make the most of it. You can be sure they'll want to know everything about Patten Roberts." Ivy looked at Wallis with concern.

"Don't worry. I'm ready for them," Wallis returned confidently. "As a matter of fact, I'm looking forward to it." Wallis glanced at her tank watch, noting that it was nearly one o'clock. "In the meantime, I'd better get ready for Chief Johnson. He should be here any minute."

Ivy rose to go. "That just about covers everything. I'll let you know when the chief arrives." She was about to turn and head for the door, but she stopped for just a moment. "And Wallis—"

The beautiful young mayor didn't let her finish the sentence. "I know, I know. I'm going to finish my lunch. Scout's honor." She raised two fingers as a pledge and quickly took another bite of the sandwich.

For the next hour and a half, Wallis met with the

chief of police and the executive committee of the chamber of commerce. The meetings were perfunctory introductions, each organization formally laying out its problems and goals. Wallis knew it was important that they start out on the right foot, and so she tried to listen with an open mind to each representative without bringing any preconceived biases to the discussions. She had campaigned on the premise that government was people, not machines, and while she knew that there were powerful groups at work behind the scenes, she was determined to listen to individual needs and concerns. By the time Graham Davis was ushered into her spacious office a little before three, she had made a good start in establishing good working relationships with the two groups.

"Good afternoon, Graham. It's good to see you again." She met him at the door and clasped his hand warmly, motioning him to sit down in one of the large leather chairs grouped casually at one side of the room. She was truly glad to see her friend; she knew that she could relax and be herself with this man, since they shared many of the same dreams and aspirations. He was a powerful ally.

"It's good of you to find time for me today," he answered. "I imagine you're beginning to get a good taste of the rigorous schedule of this office—though I don't suppose there have been many surprises for you."

Wallis laughed good-naturedly as she sat down in a chair next to him. Instinctively she knew this was no time to sit behind the desk. "Oh, I'm sure there will be plenty of surprises for me along the way. I've got my share of experience, but it's not possible to know everything there is to know. But one thing I do know for sure is that there's always time on my schedule for you. Now, what brings you here?"

"Well, it's about Patten Roberts," the distinguished-looking city councilman began. He stopped for a moment and looked Wallis straight in the eye, as if he were trying to decide how to finish his sentence. Wallis gave a nod of understanding, and this seemed to be the signal he was looking for.

"Look, Wallis. I don't want you to think I'm being patronizing, because I'm really not. It's just that—" he hesitated just a moment, "I think you must be certain of this man. You need to be sure he's the man you want."

"Graham, there's something you're not telling me. I need to have *all* the facts," she urged softly.

"Oh, I know you do. That's why I'm here. You know you've got my support. Ernie is going to do everything in his power to block this nomination. He said out loud to us all this morning as we were leaving the council that Patten Roberts was, and I quote, 'a pipsqueak who didn't know up from down.'"

"Now that's what I call a well-informed opinion," Wallis said bitterly, interrupting him.

But Graham wasn't to be cut short. "That's not all. He also asked Ellie if she didn't agree that Patten Roberts was too young for the job. Ellie, of course, agreed with him wholeheartedly. She always does. I guess that's about it, except that there's a general feeling among the Old Guard that he's an outsider coming in to rearrange their city." Graham paused for a moment, giving Wallis a chance to speak.

"Graham, you know me well enough to know that I wouldn't have nominated Patten Roberts if I didn't have complete faith in his ability. And I expected as much from Ernie—and Ellie, too, for that matter. If those two are our only problems, we're in good shape. I can do battle with Ernie, if it comes to that. Don't forget, I know how he operates. Tell me—what about Papadakis?"

Wallis was very much interested in what Graham had to say, and for the next several minutes the two allies discussed Patten Roberts' nomination, Graham giving his view of the various council members and Wallis explaining what she expected from each, as well as her strategies for securing the nomination.

"This has been a great help," Wallis finally said. "I really do appreciate your coming to see me. I think I have a better idea now of what's to come, but I feel confident we'll win this round. In the final analysis, Roberts is the best in the country. That's all that matters." She stood up, signaling the end of the meeting. "I don't mean to rush you off, but I've got an appointment at three-thirty—with a bear. Two, in fact."

Graham Davis grinned as he stood up. "The pandas, right?"

"You got it," Wallis confirmed, returning his smile. The two of them walked to the door. "Actually, I'm looking forward to it. It'll be great to get outside for a change." Her hand was on the door knob, but she turned to her friend again. "I can't tell you how grateful I am for your help. I know how busy you are."

"I'm just glad we had a chance to talk. I was a little afraid that you might take offense at my frankness. I didn't want you to think I had any doubts myself about the nomination, because I don't. I'm behind you all the way. As far as I'm concerned, you couldn't have picked a better man than Patten Roberts."

"Listen, Graham. You and I have worked together for a long time, and I have great respect for your opinion. Just because I'm mayor now doesn't mean I don't want to hear what you have to say." She opened the door. "I don't see how I can go wrong with you in my corner."

After Graham thanked her cordially and left, Wallis returned to her desk, picked up the phone and called the receptionist. "Hello, Phyl. Is Ivy still here?" She was silent for just a moment, her beautifully polished nails tapping restlessly on the smooth surface of her desk. "No, no. That's all right. I'll see her there. Thanks anyway." She hung up the phone, staring thoughtfully at her hand still resting on the receiver.

With a sigh, she got up from her desk and went to the tiny bathroom that adjoined her office. Glancing in the mirror, she got out her hairbrush and brushed her hair until it fell naturally on her shoulders in a gentle flip. The little bit of makeup that she wore—a touch of light brown eye shadow, a bit of rose blush—was fine. All she needed was to freshen up her lipstick, and she was ready to go.

Wallis made her way through the busy front office, taking just a few moments to speak to her staff members. She was genuinely interested in each of them and she had allowed herself a few minutes' extra time. She didn't want to be the kind of politician who didn't have time for people. Once outside the office, she went directly to the elevators that led to the underground parking. It was impossible for her to walk through the building without being recognized, and she found herself exchanging greetings with several passersby as she made her way to her yellow Mustang convertible—a vintage car and her pride and joy.

There had been a big ruckus when she had refused to have a driver or a city car, and as she pulled out of the parking lot into the startlingly blue afternoon, she was glad that she had insisted on her own transportation. She didn't like to be dependent on anyone else for anything, and she valued the freedom that came from being on her own.

The top was down on the convertible and her long hair blew softly around her face. Stopping at a red light, she reached into the glove compartment and got out a yellow silk scarf. Most of the time she didn't mind the wind-blown look, but since she knew reporters were waiting, she thought she'd better pay some attention to her appearance. When the light changed to green, she pressed down on the accelerator, checking her watch for the correct time. She still had twenty minutes so she relaxed, turning over in her mind the information Graham had given her. The convertible moved smoothly through the traffic as she headed toward the zoo. Actually, Graham had told her nothing that she hadn't already expected, but it was good to have confirmation. Linc Washington was the only council member whose reactions Graham couldn't predict—this was his first term on the council—but Wallis was having lunch with him the next day. She would sound him out then.

Her mind was busy with the nomination of Patten Roberts as she drove down Montrose past the Museum of Fine Arts and circled Mecom Fountain. She didn't see the motorcycle come up behind her. In fact, she wouldn't even have noticed the biker as he passed her if he hadn't called out her name. And even then, catching a glimpse of him out of the corner of her eye, she didn't recognize him at first, not consciously. It wasn't until he pulled up next to the convertible that she realized who he was—the stranger on the rooftop! She couldn't believe her eyes. He grinned impishly and, with a roguish wave, spun off into the park.

"What on earth—" Wallis sputtered. Just at that moment, when she might have followed him, a Mercedes suddenly moved from the far lane and cut in front of her so that she had to swerve to avoid being hit, the squeal of the tires a shrill indication of a very close call. By the time Wallis had her bearings, the motorcycle and its handsome driver were nowhere to be seen. Another red light delayed her again, and as she drove into the park, she had no hope of finding him.

He saw me, she puzzled to herself. Why didn't he slow down? But of course, he probably didn't even remember losing his cigarette case. For all she knew, he had a dozen of them—which meant that if he didn't know she had his case, he'd had no reason to stop. What, she wondered, was he doing, riding around in the middle of the afternoon like a teen-ager?

She was still thinking all of this to herself as she pulled into the parking lot next to the zoo, but she had little faith in her own rationalizations. She knew he wasn't the kind of person who would have a dozen silver cigarette cases engraved with his initials. And she knew intuitively that he was something special.

Oh, well, she said to herself with resignation as she opened the car door and stepped out, glancing at her watch, this is no time to start daydreaming again. I've got work to do, and I have no intention of being so easily distracted. But in spite of herself, a dark cloud seemed to have settled over her, and her good spirits of a few minutes earlier were considerably diminished.

When she saw him again, inside the zoo, she was not even surprised. He was standing across from the lions' cage, buying a sack of popcorn and wearing a khaki trenchcoat over tan trousers, a yellow oxford cloth button-down shirt, and a tan cashmere pullover sweater. He looked up in her direction, smiled when he saw her, and waved. His blue eyes twinkled, and his careless blond hair was golden in the sunlight. In spite of the layers of winter clothing, there was no hiding the masculine strength of his lean, muscular frame. His eyes met Wallis's with unflinching candor, and she realized he had been waiting for her.

As she approached the entrance to the zoo, she felt the sensuous scrutiny of his gaze as surely as if he had run his fingers gently over her body, and a thrill of anticipation shot through her.

"Greetings, Your Honor," he said with an engaging grin.

Wallis nodded. "We meet again." Her voice was soft and her wide amber eyes met his directly.

"Here, have some popcorn," he said, holding out the sack.

"Thanks," she said, taking a handful. "I believe I will."

"Did you think we wouldn't?" he asked, putting the change in his pocket.

"What? Meet again?" Wallis put a kernel of popcorn in her mouth. "To tell you the truth, I've been counting on it," she added, a little mysteriously.

"So have I," he countered, "I've never doubted that we would." His tone of voice and the gleam in his eyes left no doubt as to his meaning.

Wallis wisely chose not to pick up on the flirtatious implications of his words. Instead, she reached into her pocket for the silver cigarette case. "I believe this is yours," she said, holding out the case to him.

"So *you've* got it," he said, obviously elated. "I wondered where I'd left it." He took the case from her and playfully tossed it into the air a couple of times.

"I thought you'd be glad to see it. It looks like a very fine cigarette case." Wallis couldn't help commenting on his obvious pleasure.

"Oh, I am. And it is," he said, putting the case into his pants pocket. "It was a present," he explained unnecessarily.

"Is she very beautiful?" Wallis asked lightly, a little surprised at her own audacious inquiry. She knew that she would be late if she stayed much longer, but it seemed impossible for her to tear her eyes away from his. It was as though she were responding to some kind of magnetism against which she was powerless. Besides, she didn't even know his name. She couldn't leave without that—she just couldn't.

"*Very* beautiful," he said, taking her by the arm and leading her toward the petting zoo. "And if you don't hurry, you're going to be late. And I don't want to be responsible for that."

Wallis was more than a little taken aback. "How do you know I'm about to be late?" she asked, genuinely puzzled. It was useless to do anything but walk with him, and she enjoyed the touch of his strong hand on her arm.

"There's not much I don't know about you," he replied, looking down at her with a grin.

"That's a little one-sided, don't you think?" Wallis bristled. "I don't even know your name." They were walking past the monkeys, heading toward the petting zoo. He seemed to know where she was going.

"No, I guess you don't," he said, looking down at

her, his blue eyes searching hers for a moment as if he were deciding whether or not he should tell her. "But that's easily remedied." They were approaching the group of dignitaries and reporters. "Davenport, Sam Davenport."

Wallis stopped short and looked at him in astonishment. The truth began to dawn on her. "Not Sam Davenport—the journalist who won a Pulitzer Prize for that series of articles on nursing homes?" As she spoke, she pulled her arm free of his grasp.

"One and the same," Sam said with a little bow. "At your service."

A wave of shock and fury swept through her body. She might have known he was a reporter—no doubt looking for a good story. And this was not just any reporter. This was one of the top investigative journalists in the country. To think she had believed, even for a moment, that he was interested in her as a person! She felt as if she'd been slapped in the face. But Wallis was entirely too professional to forget about the crowd of onlookers. She wasn't about to let her feelings betray her at that moment—not when every eye was on her. Out of the corner of her eye, she could see Ivy walking toward her with a man she assumed was Mr. Tsien. Summoning every ounce of discipline she had, she smiled graciously, if a bit coolly, and extended her hand to him.

"You have quite a reputation, Mr. Davenport," she said icily, "for getting a story regardless of the cost. No doubt you already have one in mind—" But before she could finish, Ivy was at her side, and Mr. Tsien was greeting her enthusiastically.

Her natural poise and graciousness helped her through the next several minutes, and no one looking at the charming mayor could guess at her emotional turmoil. Acutely conscious of Sam Davenport's eyes on her, she turned her full attention to her mayoral duties.

Ivy had everything well under control, of course, and after formal introductions, Wallis and the Chinese delegation moved over to the small portable stage that had been erected for the occasion, stopping first to pose for photographers and to walk through the low-fenced enclosure to visit for a moment with the pandas, who were already comfortably ensconced in their new quarters. Wallis knew that she had to get through this occasion. Sam Davenport was just another reporter doing his job, nothing more. When the ceremonies finally were over and she and Mr. Tsien had both given short, prepared speeches, Wallis began mentally preparing for the questions from the press. It looked as if reporters from every local newspaper, magazine, and television station were there. Wallis knew most of them by name and had no qualms about what was ahead.

After saying good-bye to the Chinese dignitaries, she returned to the stage and microphone. The reporters were waiting, pencils in hand, and the photographers were again busy taking pictures.

"Why did you nominate Patten Roberts—?"

"Is it true that you drive your own—?"

"Will you oversee the—?"

They all started at once but Wallis stopped them

with a wave of her hand. When all was quiet, she pointed to Blake Daniels, a reporter from the *News* who had covered her campaign. She knew he could be counted on for a thoughtful question.

"Mr. Daniels?"

"Why did you nominate Patten Roberts? How can someone from the East understand our traffic problems here in the Southwest? Aren't the problems very different?"

Wallis didn't hesitate a moment. "Yes, indeed, they are very different. That's one of the main reasons I nominated Patten Roberts. He grew up in Dallas and majored in architecture at the University of Texas at Austin before going on to graduate school at Harvard. So he's a native Texan and can bring us the best of both worlds." She smiled at Blake and turned to acknowledge another reporter, carefully avoiding Sam Davenport, who was lounging against a fence, eating popcorn. She knew he would have a question for her sooner or later, but this was her terrain, and she was once again back on solid footing. She could handle it, and she could handle him.

"Do you expect any difficulty in securing this appointment?" asked a woman from a suburban paper. "Ellie Johnson says he's too young for the job. How do you answer that?"

Wallis grinned. "Mr. Roberts is thirty-five years old—a year older than I am, though I suppose that won't be very reassuring in some quarters." She got the laugh she was hoping for and when the friendly chuckles died down, she began again in a more serious tone. "All kidding aside, Mr. Roberts has been director of mass transit systems in Baltimore for the last seven years and before that an assistant director in Los Angeles. Both cities have formidable transit problems, and his record in both was brilliant. I'm convinced he has the best credentials in the country."

For the next twenty minutes or so, Wallis answered questions about Patten Roberts and that day's city council meeting. After that, the rest of the questions were relatively easy, concerned mostly with the police department and city services, and Wallis fielded those with no difficulty. Glancing at her watch she saw that it was getting late, and she was about to close the press conference when a familiar voice spoke out from the back. She looked up just in time to see Sam Davenport crumple the empty popcorn sack.

"Ms. Mayor, what do you know about the Gulf Coast Development Corporation?" A respectful hush fell over the reporters as Sam Davenport asked his question. When he spoke, people listened, and it was obvious that this was what he expected as he continued in his soft, masculine drawl. "Are you prepared to deal with a scandal that might affect your administration?" His blue eyes gave no quarter as he watched her face, waiting for an answer.

Wallis had not even heard of the Gulf Coast Development Corporation, and her heart sank a little. Her customary self-confidence came to the forefront, however, and she wisely decided this was no time for false pride. Instead, she said quite frankly, "I'm not familiar with the, what did you say, the Gulf Coast—" she faltered.

"Development Corporation," he finished, without looking in her direction. He was tossing the popcorn sack into a nearby waste container.

"Thank you, Mr. Davenport. Gulf Coast Development Corporation is something I know nothing about, but I can assure you that I'm not afraid of scandal. This administration has nothing to hide, and while I have to wonder at the implications of your question, I can assure you that if there is a scandal, it will be dealt with openly and honestly. Perhaps if you have information that would be of interest to this administration, you will share it with us."

At that point, Ivy stepped forward and took the microphone from Wallis. There would be more questions but the chief aide would answer them, giving Wallis a chance to slip away.

As she walked through the zoo toward her car, she pondered that last question. What on earth was the Gulf Coast Development Corporation and what kind of scandal could possibly threaten her administration? She was confident that Sam Davenport asked no idle questions, and she was bound and determined to get to the bottom of all this. She made a mental note to put Ivy to work on it first thing in the morning. She didn't like to think that Sam Davenport knew something that she didn't.

Wallis was so preoccupied with her thoughts that this time she really wasn't expecting to see Sam Davenport again. So she was completely caught off guard when she rounded the corner and walked into the parking lot. He was bent over looking at the tires of her car. As she approached the yellow convertible, he gave the front right tire one more kick before he brushed his hands together and leaned against the car, obviously waiting for her. The grin on his face gave every indication that he was pleased with himself.

"You know, if this keeps up, I may have to reconsider my decision about having a driver," Wallis said drily, as she took out her car keys and prepared to unlock the door. She was determined to act as if nothing extraordinary was happening.

"You took the words right out of my mouth," Sam drawled. And without waiting for her to reply, he easily took the keys from her hand.

"What are—?" Wallis protested. But it was too late. He had taken her by the arm and was walking her around to the other side of the car.

"You said you wanted to know about the Gulf Coast Development Corporation. I'm going to oblige you." He grinned at her as he unlocked the car door. "And I thought maybe we'd have a bite to eat." He was holding the door open for her.

That did it. Wallis's curiosity got the better of her. It was live bait and she went for it. "That's a hard invitation to resist," she answered, "but then I guess you already knew that, didn't you?" She studied him for a moment, weighing the alternatives. "And the beautiful woman? Will she object?"

Sam grinned. "Hardly! My aunt lives in Rhode Island with twenty-three cats and a bird dog. She hasn't been to Texas in years."

Wallis had to laugh—she'd been had and she knew it. He had the key to her car and the information she wanted. What else could she do?

"Let's go," she said, getting into the car. "I'm starved." As long as she remembered that he was just another reporter out for a story, she would be all right—she thought.

3

Where are you taking me?" Wallis asked a trifle suspiciously as Sam turned the car down a narrow street in the warehouse district slightly north of downtown. She had always thought that she knew the downtown area like the back of her hand, but this particular section was unfamiliar territory. She tugged at her neat black silk bow tie, thinking how strange it felt to be a passenger in her own car. For a moment she almost wished that she was at home in her old bathrobe, curled up on the sofa with a bowl of popcorn. But there was something about Sam that captured her curiosity, that made her want to see what he would do next.

"You mean you don't know?" Sam teased. "Why, you're the mayor, and you mean you haven't been to one of the best Mexican restaurants in the city?"

Wallis was indignant. "I could have tried to eat my way through all the Mexican restaurants in the city, and I still wouldn't have discovered them all, even after all the time I've been here. And I certainly wouldn't think to look for one in this deserted area."

"Ah, but that's part of its charm," Sam said softly. The deep voice sent shivers through Wallis. "The charm of the unexpected."

He would like that, Wallis reflected. After all, that was what she liked about him—the charm of the unexpected. She should have known, from that first moment with Sam on the roof the night of her inauguration, that he would reappear unexpectedly. She felt herself succumbing to the charm of the man and the evening, and she knew that she was going to have to pull in, gather her resources. She was still having a hard time forgiving Sam for not telling her sooner that he was a reporter, but she knew she was being unreasonable. They had, after all, just met. She kept remembering the feeling of being held in his arms, of his lips on hers, and she knew that these thoughts could only lead to trouble. As it was, she was all too aware of him next to her, of his strong hands gripping the steering wheel. A bit cross with herself as well as with him, she said gruffly, "Well, it certainly will be unexpected, that's for sure."

"But charming," Sam insisted.

"Maybe," she agreed a little reluctantly and then hurried on. "But I didn't come to dinner with you for the sake of charm. I thought you said you had some information that could be useful to me. You did say you knew something about the Gulf Coast Development Corporation."

They had stopped for a red light, and Wallis could see silver highlights in his blond hair as the late afternoon sun fell behind the buildings. He chuckled, a low, throaty sound that made Wallis look at him curiously. He gave her a quick smile before driving on. "That I do," he said matter-of-factly. "That I do."

"Then what's so funny?" Wallis asked. She didn't get laughed at very often, and she wasn't sure she liked it now, although there had been something about the sound of that chuckle that had unaccountably pleased her.

"You are. All business. Doesn't the mayor have a lighter side, a personal life? Is it really all work, work, work? I seem to recall a certain beautiful evening on a rooftop not very far from here . . ."

Wallis flushed, if only because his thoughts so closely paralleled her own. "That was then and this is now. After all, the only reason I came tonight was to talk about the Gulf Coast Development Corporation and what it has to do with my administration. I don't like being the last to know things, especially when they involve this city."

Sam smoothly pulled the car into a parking space outside what appeared to be another warehouse. "Is that really the only reason you came tonight, Wallis?" Without giving her a chance to answer, he got out of the car and came around to her side, opening the door and extending a hand to her. As he pulled her up next to him—too close for comfort, Wallis thought—his blue eyes suddenly shot sparks and he said quickly, "Because if that's the only reason, you're just going to have to wait. When I'm ready to tell you, I'll tell you. After dinner. Not during, and not before."

Wallis looked up at him and, seeing the expression in his eyes, knew that it would be useless to press the point. "All right then," she conceded. "After dinner."

As if some bargain had been struck between them, Sam gave her hand, which he still held in his own, a squeeze, then led her to a door in the long stucco wall of the building. He knocked, then stood back, apparently waiting for entry. Wallis, puzzled by the entire proceeding, could only look on in amusement and amazement as a peephole opened in the door, and a pair of bright brown eyes looked them over. Quickly the peephole closed, and the door was opened for them.

A tall, good-looking man stood in the doorway, and his brown eyes twinkled with humor as he pulled his neat black mustache. "Ah, Señor Davenport," he said with a broad smile. "Back again so soon? But I see that you are doing us a tremendous honor tonight. Granted, we have served dinner to many dignitaries, but never to one so beautiful."

Sam smiled and shook hands with the man, while Wallis blushed a bit at the compliment, though she had expected to be recognized no matter where they went for dinner. It went with the job. And this man seemed nice enough, and so did his restaurant. Over his shoulder, she could see the inviting interior of the place—a large bar built of glass bricks and lit by colorful neon lights. The sounds of mariachi music were coming from a brightly lit jukebox, and Wallis could see a few men standing alongside the bar, playing their own instruments in time to the music.

She looked up at Sam's face to see a broad smile. "See?" he asked proudly. "I told you it was charming. So why are we standing out here?"

"Why indeed?" asked the tall man, standing aside and beckoning them in. "Allow me to introduce myself. I'm Antonio Garcia, the owner of the Last Concert, and I can only welcome you, Your Honor, and say that we're pleased to have you with us."

"I'm very pleased to meet you," Wallis returned graciously, shaking hands with him. "What a wonderful place this is!" And she meant it. Everywhere she looked there were people laughing and talking and eating—the restaurant had an air of holiday celebration about it, and she was glad that Sam had brought her here. But despite looks of recognition, no one seemed inclined to bother her, and she looked forward to a relaxing dinner.

Antonio led them to a secluded table near the glass doors overlooking the central terrace, which was lush with potted plants and where several outdoor picnic tables were placed, deserted now in the cold weather. Still, Wallis could imagine what it would be like to eat outdoors in the starry night in warmer weather. She and Sam had no sooner taken their

seats than Antonio reappeared with two large glasses, both rimmed with salt, obviously containing
margaritas. "On the house!" he insisted, as Wallis
made a deprecating gesture. "To welcome you to the
Last Concert."

She had no choice but to accept with good grace,
and Antonio drifted away, after inquiring if the table
was to their liking. Sam raised his glass to hers in a
toast. "To your first visit here," he said softly, "I hope
it's only the first of many."

"Thank you." Wallis smiled. "If the food is as
pleasing as the atmosphere, I'm sure it will be,
though I doubt I could find it again without a guide."

Sam smiled. "That's part of its charm. And I
volunteer to be your guide any time you'd like." His
blue eyes met hers, and Wallis knew that this was no
casual invitation. Despite his offhand manner, there
seemed to be nothing at all casual about Sam
Davenport. All too conscious of his scrutiny, Wallis
drank deeply of her margarita, savoring the salty
tequila and lime, and she felt the tension of the day
draining from her body, leaving her relaxed and
calm. She did deserve an evening off, after all. Even
though they would have to talk about the Gulf Coast
Development Corporation sooner or later, she resolved to let Sam take his own good time. For the
moment, she was content to enjoy herself.

She looked about, savoring the festive scene, and
wondered where the waiter could be. "What about
menus?" she asked curiously, and Sam laughed in
response.

"There are very few choices here," he said, smiling. "Small or large, nachos or no nachos, and what to drink." He sat back and looked at her over the rim of his drink, his searching blue eyes taking in every aspect of her appearance.

Wallis smiled in return, enjoying his appreciative stare. Two could play at this game. "That's easy. I'll stick to my margarita, have nachos, and a large."

"That's the spirit." Sam grinned. "I like women with hearty appetites."

"I also have a hearty appetite for information," Wallis said wryly, attempting to remind him of why they were there in the first place. "Remember?"

"Oh, all right." Sam grimaced, making a show of his capitulation. "But if we talk about it now, will you promise to relax and have a good time afterwards?"

"I'll try," Wallis agreed cautiously, "but it all depends on what you have to tell me."

"Okay," Sam agreed. "I got a tip the other day, a good one. I won't bother going into who or why right this minute. That's not important. What is important is that my informer is reliable. To start from the beginning, Gulf Coast Development Corporation has been getting city contracts now for nearly twenty years."

"So?" Wallis interjected. "That hardly sounds scandalous."

"No, it's not, except for a few minor details." There was a trace of sarcasm in his voice. "They don't always do what they say they're going to do. A big contract will call for a building, let's say, for the community college, a building and two parking lots. What happens is that only one parking lot is built. There was never room for two parking lots in the first place, so no one notices. No one complains. A little here, a little there. Over the years, it adds up. Why, I even found a bridge that was never built over a dead-end street that was never completed. You multiply that sort of thing by twenty years, and we're talking big bucks."

"What?" Wallis was incredulous. "Do you have any proof?"

"Not enough. Not yet. But I'm working on it. A friend who's a private eye is helping me track down a couple leads. We'll come up with something soon enough. Don't worry."

Wallis shook her head doubtfully. "I can see it happening once or twice. But year after year? That's hard to believe." She paused thoughtfully. "Unless—"

"Right," Sam continued. "It all smells of some back-street deal, and my guess is that someone on the city payroll is involved. That's what I'm after. Nailing the Gulf Coast Development Corporation won't accomplish anything unless we find out who's behind it."

"It doesn't sound good, I have to admit," Wallis conceded, "but you don't really have all the facts—it seems to me that you're jumping to some pretty strong conclusions."

Sam leaned over the platter of steaming nachos that had been placed on the table and carefully selected one. "Maybe so, maybe so. That's why I'm ready to play a little game, to see if I can smoke out some rats."

Wallis didn't like the sound of that at all. "And what might your little game be?" She reached for a nacho herself and took her time with it, trying to think.

"Oh, nothing much," Sam said airily. "Just thought I might plant a little story about the Gulf Coast Development Corporation, see who runs for cover. Might be interesting, don't you think?"

Wallis was too shrewd a politician to be in favor of this plan. "Interesting?" she asked contemptuously. "Is that all you journalists think about? Anything for a by-line, I suppose." She was being unjust, she realized, and she made an effort to tone down her advice. "I'm sorry. That wasn't fair. I just think you should wait and get all the facts before you start jumping to conclusions." Mentally she made a note to get Ivy to work on this problem first thing the next morning, but she wasn't about to let Sam know that.

"Always the politician, aren't you?" Sam grinned. But much to her surprise, he offered no argument. "Okay," he agreed pleasantly, "if that's the way you feel about it, that's what I'll do. Wait and get all the facts. God knows, the other way would probably be quicker and easier, but I'll do whatever you think is right—you're the mayor, after all."

Wallis hadn't expected him to give in so easily and she was immediately suspicious. "You mean that's that? You won't do it until you have something more substantial to go on?"

The food came and Sam began eating, but not until he had ordered another round of margaritas. "Yes, Your Honor," he said softly. "That's that. With a couple of conditions."

Now we get to the heart of the matter, Wallis thought to herself, realizing she had been set up. Who was this man to think that he could insist on concessions from her? "And just what might those be?"

"First, that you get started on these delicious enchiladas." Sam gestured with his fork. "That's it, go ahead, eat." As Wallis began to taste her food, he continued, "Second, knowing you, you'll have that brilliant assistant of yours, Ivy Tucker, hard at work on the Gulf Coast Development Corporation first thing in the morning. Am I right?" Wallis, taken by surprise, could only nod. "Okay, then what I want is a share in the information when she gets it. And I'll share mine with her. Then, when the story breaks, when we put it all together, I'd like a break, a little lead time so I can have a headstart on the other guys."

Wallis swallowed a mouthful of delicious cheese enchilada, washed it down with a sip of her drink, and extended her hand across the table. "You've got a deal."

Much to her surprise, Sam turned her hand over and kissed it, his lips caressing her palm gently, teasingly. "You haven't heard all the conditions yet."

Wallis, tingling from the brief contact, wondered what was coming next. "All right," she said warily. "What else?"

Sam grinned, his blue eyes lighting with mischief. "Settle back and enjoy this evening."

Wallis brightened considerably at his words, having expected some impossible demand. "You drive a hard bargain, Sam Davenport."

"Only when it's worth it." The words had another meaning beyond the simple context of their conversation and Sam knew it, and Wallis knew that he knew it. There was no enmity, no feeling of suspicion between them. Every instinct she possessed told Wallis that she could trust this man, and she had felt that way about very few individuals in her lifetime. Not that she was suspicious by nature, but all her life she had been guarded and careful. It seemed that Sam deserved her trust. And she determined to give it to him.

Dinner flew by after their business was settled, and Wallis found herself relaxing and talking to Sam as if they were old friends. "You know all about me, it seems," she said a bit defensively, "but I know very little about you, beyond the fact you've won a Pulitzer. So . . ."

"You mean you want to know where I've been all your life?" The question would have been arrogant coming from anyone else, but Sam softened it with a smile.

Wallis blushed, afraid that he realized how attracted she was to him. "Not exactly. Well, yes." She was angry at herself. Usually poised and articulate, she was painfully aware that there was something about this man that could reduce her to the status of a star-struck adolescent.

"I've been all over the country, here and there, always on the trail of a story. I've worked for AP, UPI, and several national magazines—even put in a stint in Vietnam. But life on the road is not without its problems, and I decided it was time to settle down. As a matter of fact, I've started writing a novel, and this city seems to be as good a place to work as any. I've got friends here, and a sister. Besides, the Southwest has a kind of freshness and energy that I like. Raw nerve can get a person places here."

"That's right," Wallis said impishly, tension gone for the moment. "Look where it got me!"

They both laughed, and then Sam's expression became very serious. "Hardly," he said, and there was a tone of respect in his voice. "You have a lot more going for you than just raw nerve. You have background and experience and you've done your homework. I think you have a bright future in politics, Wallis, and I think you deserve every bit of recognition that comes your way. You've worked hard."

Wallis was touched by the admiration and the undercurrent of understanding that ran through his words. She decided to accept the compliment gracefully. "Thank you."

"And one more thing," Sam added, the teasing note back in his voice. "You're the sexiest woman in politics in this country today."

"Enough of that," Wallis insisted. "Something tells me that's not an entirely professional judgment."

"Right you are," Sam agreed. Having finished his dinner he leaned back in his chair and drained the

last of his drink. "It's a very personal—and hasty—
one at that. But I intend to see a lot of you, Wallis
Carmichael—both personally and professionally."
There was a tone in his voice that Wallis could not
ignore. The man wanted her.

And, she realized with a shock, she wanted the
man. She wanted to spend time with him, wanted to
feel his lips on hers again. She took a last sip and
reflected on the hopelessness of the situation. Tonight was rare for her. It was one of the few nights
that wasn't solidly booked by some civic event and
she hadn't felt honor bound to work late in the office.
How many nights like this would she have over the
next two years? Not enough. Not nearly enough.
Looking Sam straight in the eye, she said coolly,
"I'm afraid you'll have to stand in line. Aside from
tonight, it seems that everyone in this city wants to
see a lot of me—all the time."

"Oh, but I've done my homework," Sam said
softly. "I know that you stay up late, that you love
old movies and popcorn. Besides, I have a very
flexible schedule, even if you don't. Plus, as you'll
learn, I'm the soul of discretion. I'm not after a story
with you—if I were, I'd already have one for the
National Enquirer. I kissed the mayor at her inaugural ball, and she didn't even know my name." His
tone was teasing, but Wallis knew that what he said
was true. She toyed with her napkin nervously, not
knowing quite what to say.

"So how about it?" he asked.

"How about what?"

"An old movie and popcorn. We could go to a theater, if you like."

Resolving to enjoy the evening after all, Wallis almost surprised herself by her next comment. "How about my place?"

Sam didn't bat an eye. "Fine."

They left the restaurant quickly, complimenting Antonio on the food and the service, and Wallis promised to come again. As they walked out into the cool night, Wallis found that she was actually looking forward to going home with Sam. It had been so long—too long—since she'd had a man in her house, and she realized that her life was just a bit lonely. She laughed, wondering what Sam would think of her collection of old movies, and Sam looked at her quizzically as he settled himself behind the wheel. "What's so funny?"

"Oh, you'll see," Wallis couldn't resist the urge to tease him just a bit. "You'll see."

As they pulled up in front of her bungalow in Montrose, Wallis hoped that everything would be in order, and for a moment she wondered about the wisdom of her decision. But as she walked to the door, hand in hand with Sam, she felt a surge of rebellion. This was the right thing to do. She was entitled to a few minutes of stolen pleasure. She had to relax and take it easy. After all, that's what Ivy was always telling her to do. She took a deep breath as she opened the door. "Welcome—chez Carmichael awaits you—along with the best selection of old movies you'll probably ever run across."

Sam's eyes blinked as he took in the scene, the comfortable white furniture in the living room, the colorful movie posters that lined the walls, the video recorder and television that stood on the large built-in bookshelves. "You aren't kidding." He wandered over to the bookshelves as Wallis made her way to the kitchen.

She called to him from the doorway. "Make yourself at home. I'll see to the popcorn. As a matter of fact, you might as well pick out a movie—I've seen them all, so we'll let tonight be your choice."

She loaded popcorn into the chute of the hot-air popper and went through to the bedroom to change from her suit, donning blue jeans and an old sweatshirt. Wouldn't do to get too dressed up, she thought to herself. Going back to the kitchen, she found that the popcorn was almost ready, and she loaded a wicker tray with two cans of root beer, a salt shaker, and the popcorn, which was now liberally laced with butter. As an afterthought, she added two paper napkins, though when she was alone, she usually tended to wipe her buttery fingers on her bathrobe.

"Voilà!" she said as she entered the living room in time to see Sam snapping a tape into the machine. "I see you've made your choice and I'm here with the refreshments, so let's watch a movie!"

Sam stood there for a long moment in silence, his blue eyes surveying her from head to toe, obviously taking in the trim-fitting jeans and bright pink sweatshirt. "I like you that way," he said finally. "Informality suits you, I think."

"Thanks." Wallis grinned as she placed the tray on the table and curled up on the sofa. "But I hardly think it suits the office. Suits suit the office."

"Maybe so," Sam admitted. "But it's nice to see you looking so relaxed."

And Wallis realized that she was truly relaxed. She reached for the small bowls and started dumping popcorn into them, then snapped the tabs on the cans of root beer. "And our feature tonight?" She cast an inquisitive glance in Sam's direction.

Sam stood before the television and took a bow. "Our feature tonight," he said in a parody of an announcer, "will be *Casablanca*."

"My favorite!" Wallis cried delightedly. It was a terribly romantic movie, and it always made her cry. She could never understand how Ingrid Bergman could bear to tear herself away from Humphrey Bogart.

Sam came over and sat next to her, helping himself to a bowl of popcorn and a root beer. "Is that all right?" he asked a trifle anxiously.

"Fine," Wallis assured him. "It really is one of my favorites."

"Well, there are certainly enough to choose from," he said, gently teasing her. "You have quite a collection there."

"I know," Wallis answered. "I like to think of it as my secret vice, though I suppose it's really not so secret after all."

"My lips are sealed," Sam promised solemnly, and they settled back into the depths of the comfortable sofa. Wallis knew almost every line of the movie by heart, and she was following it with only half her attention, for she was all too aware of Sam's proximity. She cast a glance at him out of the corner of her eye and noticed that he seemed to be watching the movie with rapt attention, though he did eventually put his bowl of popcorn down and stretch his arm across the back of the sofa to encircle her shoulders.

Wallis, tired from the long day, her mind spinning with a million thoughts, leaned a weary head against his shoulder, rejoicing in the sensation of his nearness. She had so many things to think about and it was so late, but this was one of her favorite movies.

I've never been so comfortable in my life, she thought to herself sleepily. Then she slowly became aware of warm lips grazing her hair, her ear, descending to the soft skin of her neck. "Mmmmm," she murmured, not wanting the sensation to stop. This is the best dream I've ever had, she thought again. She heard Humphrey Bogart's voice say, "We'll always have Paris," and she snuggled even deeper into the dream. She could hear the propellers of the plane starting up, she could see Bogart, Bergman in the lights of the runway and the mist, but she hadn't seen, she had *felt*, the warm mouth that came down to claim hers in a kiss that began as a tender caress and quickly deepened into passion. When Wallis felt a warm tongue dart between her parted lips, she knew that this was no dream. She knew this kiss—she'd been kissed like this before.

Her eyes opened wide, and she suddenly took in the whole scene—*Casablanca* on the television, the popcorn on the coffee table, and the warm, strong man beside her, who was gazing down at her with an expression of combined tenderness and amusement. "I hated to wake you," he said softly, looking at her with a question in his eyes.

"But you did it so nicely," Wallis said, the honest pleasure in her voice proof that she was not offended, though Sam looked strangely tentative.

He smiled down at her, his strong arms drawing her close. "Then I'll do it again." His lips came down to meet hers and Wallis moved toward him as well, delighted with the repetition of the kiss that had lingered so long in her memory. She was helpless to resist him. She didn't want to resist him. And he seemed to know it as his tongue explored her mouth with increasing urgency and insistence. The soft, moist warmth of the kiss only made Wallis want even more of him, and she returned his exploration with one of her own, her tongue searching his mouth, grazing his teeth, playing with the corners of his lips.

Sam drew back and looked at her, his arms still around her, his hands creeping under her sweatshirt to caress the soft flesh above the waistline of her jeans. Like a contented cat, Wallis curled into the circle of his embrace, and the question left his eyes as he deftly moved her body around so that they were lying alongside each other on the sofa. Wallis twisted a bit, conscious of his hard masculine form next to hers, but she knew that the last thing she wanted to do was move. He kissed her again, his mouth trailing kisses down the line of her neck, making a delicate circle around her collarbone above the neckline of her sweatshirt. His hands crept upward underneath the fabric, moving to cup her breasts, while one arm around her back drew her even closer to his body.

Wallis could feel the hard muscles of his thighs as he stretched full length next to her, and she let herself be bound to him in the warm circle of his embrace. There was no point in offering false resistance; she knew that. He did want her. And, she realized, she had wanted him ever since the first moment on the roof in the starlit night, the moment when he had first kissed her. Call it romance, call it fate, she told herself, but enjoy it, whatever it is.

"If you want me to leave now, you'd better say so." Sam's voice was gruff and his breathing was harsh.

She knew what he wanted to hear so she said it, knowing that it was what her heart—and her body—wanted. "Don't leave. Stay with me." In a single graceful movement, she stood up, reaching out a hand toward him. He stood up slowly, putting an arm around her waist, and they walked upstairs to the bedroom.

4

Wallis rolled over in bed, one reluctant eye glancing at the alarm clock. Six-thirty. She rolled back over and closed her eyes, reveling in the comfort of the soft sheets and the warmth of a bed the morning after two lovers had slept in it. Two lovers! Six-thirty!

I must be losing my mind, she thought. It's already six-thirty and this is going to be a very busy day. She usually got up well before six to do a few warm-up exercises and shower before having breakfast and heading for the office. But today she had already overslept, and what's worse, she had Sam to deal with.

Where was he anyway? Wallis looked about suspiciously for signs of his presence, but she couldn't find anything except the telltale indentation on the pillow next to hers. She threw the covers back and reached for her chenille bathrobe, tied it around her waist, and headed for the door. She could hear the sounds of a man singing in the kitchen and she started to head directly for the stairs, but something stopped her.

Looking back at the bed with its tangle of sheets and the pillows next to each other, she couldn't help but smile, a languorous smile, the smile of a woman who had been well loved the previous night and who knew it all too well. She had been surprised at herself—not only for accepting Sam's invitation to go out to dinner but for inviting him to spend the night. Nothing could have been more out of character. Ever since she had begun her career in politics, she had been more than circumspect. Oh, she had had a few affairs in law school, but nothing serious. And since her graduation she had been careful not to do anything the least bit questionable. Wallis knew that nothing could ruin a politician more quickly than a sexual scandal.

A satisfied smile played about her lips. In certain eyes, last night's behavior would surely be construed as scandalous. But it had certainly been pleasurable. Sam had followed her up the stairs in silence, both of them apparently wanting to keep the spell that had fallen between them working its magic—right up to the moment when they stood in front of Wallis's double bed.

"Are you sure about this?" Sam asked, his blue eyes searching out her amber ones, wanting to be sure that she wanted him as much as he wanted her.

He was a bit hesitant, as if he felt that he were pressuring her. But Wallis, while she appreciated the chance his question gave her to back out, had no doubts.

"Of course I'm sure," she said softly, reaching for him, putting both arms around his neck and pulling his face near hers. "But what about you?"

"It's different for me," he said softly, a smile playing about his lips as he traced the outline of her mouth with a long finger. "Tomorrow morning will be a hell of a lot easier for me than it will be for you, you know. I won't have to get up and go to City Hall and run a city council meeting."

"I don't really see that that has much to do with what's happening right now," Wallis said, though she knew the point he was trying to make. "I make an effort to keep politics out of the bedroom—or at least I'm trying to." She smiled up at him, waiting for him to make the next move. It wasn't long in coming.

Wallis stood on tiptoe to reach him as he pulled her even closer to him. When his lips came down to hers, she was ready and eager for the embrace. She should have known, ever since that romantic first meeting on the roof of the Cotton Exchange building, that romantic, wonderful night, that there was something about this man that had the power to arouse her beyond all her previous experience. The chemistry had been right from the very beginning.

The kiss was curiously gentle at first, and Sam took his time with her, as if he were testing her feelings. His tongue slid smoothly between her parted lips and gently, lazily, traced the interior of her mouth.

Wallis returned his every movement, making sure that his arousal was a mirror image of her own. When they drew apart for a brief moment, she traced a line of kisses down the strong column of his throat, loving the sensation of his pulse beating beneath her touch. She could hear his heart racing, and she knew that her own heart matched the tempo. They both felt the vibrations, she was sure of it. If she hadn't been, she would never be doing what she was doing.

Sam drew back and looked at her, a smile on his face—a tender smile, filled with true pleasure. "It seems to me that we're standing around wasting a perfectly good bed, Your Honor," he said teasingly, his blue eyes surveying her face.

"You're right, we are," she agreed, and then she made a little moue of distaste. "And don't call me that."

"No problem." He laughed; his strong fingers tickled her ribs and dropped to the flesh above the waist of her jeans, teasing the exposed skin with his touch. "I can keep politics out of the bedroom, you know. I know what belongs in the bedroom. And I especially know what belongs in this bedroom."

Wallis looked up at him with a question in her eyes. "All right—what?" she asked.

"You and me," he said softly. "We belong right here in this bedroom right now."

Wallis could only nod her agreement as his hands reached for the edge of her sweatshirt and pulled it over her head. She stood there, her bare breasts exposed, waiting to see his reaction and, for just a moment, feeling a bit timid. He quickly brought his lips down to first one nipple, then the other, teasing and tormenting her with his tongue until she ached with desire.

"Now it's my turn," she said softly, reaching for the buttons of his shirt. She was amazed at her own boldness. Never had she been so audacious, so open with a man. She had confidence in herself, and she knew that she was attractive, but she had never had the desire to use that attractiveness, not in the way that she was using it now. She knew that everything she was doing was making Sam want her even more, and she gloried in the knowledge and in the sensual confidence that was growing by the moment.

Not that she was completely in control of the situation. No matter what she did to arouse him, he retained his firm control, making sure that she was as aroused as he. When his hands slipped to the zipper of her jeans, and he slowly brought the denim length down her body, she lay back on the bed, tantalizing him deliberately.

He laughed, tracing a finger down the length of her thigh, then teased her by caressing a path upwards again, then down the other thigh, then up again, until Wallis thought that she couldn't stand it for another minute. As if he knew it, he stood back to remove the rest of his clothing, and though she reached out, he firmly but gently pushed her back on the bed, as if defying her to touch him until he wanted her to. Finally, all the restrictions of clothing were dealt with, flung to the four corners of the beautiful cinnamon-colored bedroom, and Wallis nestled back into the depths of the bedcovers, not even wanting to pull them back, not wanting to waste a minute doing something besides making love.

Sam took his time, caressing every inch of her body with his fingers and lips. Wallis lay back, luxuriating in the sensual pleasure that radiated throughout the entire room. She clutched him to her, savoring the strong scent of his masculine cologne, thinking that no other man had ever smelled so good or tasted so sweet. As she twisted away from his touch, he firmly pulled her close to him again, not letting the tension ease for a minute.

Wallis, wanting to share some of the pleasure that she was feeling, found that he tasted good all over. She explored his body with abandon, teasing the strong brown masculine nipples until they were as erect as her own. It was an awesome power she had, but she had never even known that she possessed it until Sam had made her feel so desirable.

Finally, when the tension approached the breaking point, Sam parted her legs with his own and came to her in the final embrace, the one they had both been moving toward. It was everything she had dreamed it would be. Wallis savored the feeling of his flesh entangled with her own, stroking her, teasing her, until she cried out with pleasure, a cry that was soon echoed by his own sharp exclamation of satisfaction. He collapsed on her, his full length stretched against her, and Wallis welcomed the sensation of his weight, taking it eagerly. Still joined, they both fell asleep as if neither one of them wanted to be separated, though both of them were too tired to make love again.

Wallis stood at the head of the stairs in her bathrobe, remembering, the smile still playing about her lips. They had slept in each other's arms, and when she had stirred during the night, he woke, sitting up slightly to be sure she was all right and waiting until she was comfortable again before going back to sleep himself. She was not accustomed to such caring, and the easy companionship of the night before had been a delightful surprise. It had been lovely—a night she would always remember. But it didn't look as if she would be having any more nights like that for a long time. Not if this morning was any indication. She simply didn't have the time. She didn't want a long-term relationship—not even with Sam. It wasn't part of her plan. But still, she would like to wake up with someone every morning. There was something incredibly wonderful in being able to start off the morning with such pleasant memories of the night before.

Well, it's now or never, she thought, starting down the stairs. I wonder what he's up to. As she got closer to the kitchen, she could smell coffee and frying bacon, and she could hear Sam humming "Oh, what a beautiful morning . . ." in his low voice. He's happy too, she thought. This realization gave her pleasure.

She stood at the doorway watching him. He had

found an apron in a drawer, as well as everything else he needed, for the table was laid on a bright red, white, and blue cloth and breakfast looked as delicious as it smelled. She smiled at the sight, never having had a man in her kitchen before—a man who was fixing her breakfast and doing a bang-up job of it, to all appearances.

As if he sensed her presence, Sam turned toward her, giving her a wide grin. "Breakfast is about to be served, Your Honor."

"I thought I told you not to call me that," she returned good-naturedly, giving him a quick good-morning kiss. She was determined not to linger over breakfast with him. She didn't have time and she didn't want to give Sam any false expectations. "I'll shower and get dressed," she said, pointedly looking at the clock on the wall, "and then I'll come down and grab a bite and be on my way. This is going to be a very busy day and I'm late as it is."

"Fine, go ahead," Sam said, completely unruffled. "I'll be waiting."

And he was. Wallis hurried through her shower, ran a brush through her thick hair, and dressed quickly in one of her favorite suits—a black pinstripe of severe design that she softened with a maroon silk shirt. When she came back down to the kitchen, Sam was seated, having already fixed her plate.

"Looks great," she commented, smiling as she took a seat.

"Tastes great too," he said between mouthfuls of toast and bacon. "You hurry up and eat and be off.

But give some thought to what you'd like to do tonight."

"Tonight?" Wallis asked. "I don't know about you, but I plan to spend tonight riding around the city with some of the police officers on duty. It's part of my program for better relations with the police department. And I doubt that I'll want to do anything after that, so don't make any plans including me."

Sam looked at her, reached inside the pocket of his shirt, and pulled out a business card. "Fine," he said lightly, giving her the card. "Just give me a call when you're through."

"Oh, I'll give you a call," Wallis said, and she genuinely intended to, though she doubted that she would that evening.

"Great," Sam said. "Now you go on. I'll finish up here and do the dishes. I'm sure I'll be seeing you later at the council meeting anyway. I've got a feeling this one could be newsworthy."

Wallis refused to rise to the bait, determined to handle the situation casually. "All right then, I'll see you later. Thanks for breakfast."

Sam looked up at her with a truly wicked grin. "Thanks for last night, though I have the feeling that I'll be saying that again sometime soon."

"We'll see," Wallis said, but she softened the remark with a smile. She didn't have the time to hash out any ground rules at the moment. Her mind was already out the door, in her office, preparing for the challenges of the day.

Wallis had only a few moments to check in with

Ivy before she was due at the city council meeting—
an especially important one because the council had
as its first item on the agenda the confirmation of
Patten Roberts. Wallis knew, and not just from
Graham Davis, that there was a lot of rumbling about
the appointment. She knew that the council chambers would be swarming with reporters, especially
after the questions they had asked at the zoo the day
before, and she was eager to get the meeting behind
her.

Taking a few deep breaths as she walked into the
chambers, Wallis was glad to see Graham already at
his seat. He gave her an affable smile as she went
around to her place. Ernie Dayton was puffing away
on a smelly cigar, and she noticed that he pointedly
ignored her arrival. Good, she thought, at least the
battle lines are clearly drawn. Ellie Johnson gave
Wallis a smile, but Wallis knew that she was too well
mannered to do otherwise. Papadakis, coming in
behind Ellie, said hello, and Wallis glanced around to
be sure that all fourteen members of the council were
present. Only Lamar Steele, the powerful and
wealthy philanthropist and owner of the local professional basketball team, was late, and Wallis knew that
he had called in, saying that a flat tire had delayed
him. He had already publicly endorsed Roberts, and
she fervently hoped that he would arrive soon.

As she called the meeting to order, Wallis glanced
toward the back of the room, confirming that her
sense of things had been correct and that the visitors'
gallery was filled with reporters, in addition to the

usual number of observers from various citizens' action groups and high-school civics classes. Quickly looking through the papers at her seat, she checked to make sure the agenda was there. Just as she was sitting down, she noticed two men entering the room. One, she noticed with relief, was Lamar Steele, who must have changed his flat tire in record time. The other was Sam Davenport. She could feel a quick flush rise to her cheeks, but she soon had her emotions under control. I suppose I'd better get used to this, she told herself firmly. Wallis had always had a clear notion that her work and her personal life should be two separate things, but this was the first time she was really having a chance to practice it.

"The first item on the agenda," she said calmly, "is to discuss the confirmation of Patten Roberts as director of the mass transit system." She waited to see who would be the first to speak.

Much to her surprise, Theo Papadakis began to talk. "I move that we confirm the nomination."

Wallis was grateful for his support, and she waited to see what would happen. Graham quickly said, "I second that motion."

The discussion that followed was fast and furious. Ernie, waving his cigar around the room and scattering clouds of foul-smelling smoke, was the first to object. "I just don't think that we know enough about this Patten Roberts. I don't doubt, of course, that our honorable mayor has done her homework on this issue, but I still feel that there's more to discuss than just a blanket yes or no."

Wallis had to struggle to suppress a smile as she glanced again toward the back of the room and saw Sam roll his eyes. She decided that the best course of action was to remain calm and objective. "All right, Ernie," she asked with a smile, "what do you suggest?"

"Well, I'd like to meet this boy," he said, giving her an offhand glance before he turned to his loyal ally, Ellie Johnson. "Wouldn't you, Ellie?"

Ellie nodded in agreement, and Wallis was surprised when Graham spoke up again. "Ernie, I think that's a waste of money. We've checked out his credentials; that should be enough. He's good, he's available. What if we decide to spend the money to bring him down, and then you decide you don't like him? Then we'll have to start all over again. Thank God, it's one of only a few administrative vacancies we have right now, or we'd be spending a fortune in air fares."

"Air fares will be the least of our expenses if this boy proves to be as trying and inexperienced as I'm afraid he might be. No, sir, Mr. Davis, I can't agree with you. This is no time to pinch pennies. Why, I hear this boy's going to build a bridge over downtown. And—"

"Excuse me, Mr. Dayton," Graham Davis interrupted, "but it's a monorail, not a bridge."

Ernie looked at his fellow city councilman with disdain. "Your Honor," he said sarcastically, "surely Mr. Davis doesn't have to be reminded that I have the floor. It was an oversight on his part, no doubt.

But I thank you, Mr. Davis. You've made my point. Bridge? Monorail? The truth is that I simply don't have enough information. I'd feel irresponsible if I didn't insist on knowing more before it's too late." He turned to Wallis. "Your Honor, I move that Mr. Papadakis's motion be tabled until we have a chance to meet this youngster."

No sooner had he finished speaking than Ellie was agreeing with him. "I second that motion, Your Honor."

Wallis was left no choice but to call for a vote, which was close—eight to six in favor of tabling the motion. Ernie was obviously going to have his way for a while, but while Wallis would have liked to have the nomination confirmed quickly, she wasn't at all troubled at the prospect of having Patten Roberts come to Houston.

"I move that we invite Mr. Roberts to come to Houston and meet the city council," Ernie suggested swiftly, and Ellie, as expected, seconded the motion. As if the other council members knew that this was the only way the matter could be settled, they passed it in quick order.

Wallis conceded with good grace, hoping that this would only be a temporary impediment and that once Patten Roberts had made his case in person, as it were, things would go smoothly and the confirmation would be simply a matter of routine. "Fine," she said, making a note on the legal pad before her. "I'll see that the arrangements are made. And let the record show that Mr. Dayton was wholeheartedly in favor of spending the taxpayers' money in this manner." She couldn't resist the little dig.

Fortunately, the rest of the meeting passed smoothly, and Wallis was pleased with the way the council was beginning to function as a group. When she adjourned the meeting, it was with a sense of accomplishment. She knew that she hadn't completely won the battle over Patten Roberts' confirmation, but she had no doubt that things would eventually go her way. She had faith in her ability to make decisions, and she was sure that Patten would prove himself. It would all work out.

On her way out of the city council chambers, Wallis was once again surrounded by reporters, who all seemed to sense a story in her conflict with Ernie Dayton, but Wallis certainly had no intention of giving them anything to work with. As usual, she was calm and composed and dealt with their questions easily. But out of the corner of her eye, she could see Sam Davenport deep in discussion with another reporter.

Wallis walked back to her office, weary with the morning's work but still with a long day ahead of her. Ivy popped her head in the door, asking with a gesture if Wallis wanted a cup of coffee. Wallis nodded enthusiastically, then leaned back in her chair for a few moments of relaxation.

Ivy entered with her usual steno pad, placed the coffee on the desk, and then sat down to take notes. Wallis took a deep drink of the soothing brew and leaned forward. "Two things, Ivy," she said in a matter-of-fact tone. "Schedule a trip here for Patten Roberts." She paused for a moment. "And find out everything you can about something called the Gulf Coast Development Corporation." She wanted to get to the bottom of that matter quickly—before Sam, if possible.

5

What's the hardest thing about your job?" Wallis asked Officer Ben Chaney, hoping to draw him out. It was the third Tuesday they had spent on patrol together, and there had been little time for talking. Even now it was nearly ten o'clock, and Ben would soon be taking her back downtown to the police station. Wallis couldn't help feeling that she wanted to know more about the human emotions that went with big-city police work. They had already had the usual run of events: a family brawl that had erupted into a public disturbance in a Montrose apartment house, a suspicious-looking loiterer at a nearby grocery store, a group of cars illegally parked near the zoo. Nothing serious, any of it, but Wallis had been impressed with Ben's matter-of-fact attitude that clearly indicated that this was all in a night's work. This was pretty much the way he had been for the entire three weeks she'd known him, and she wanted to know what lay beneath the surface.

Ben seemed thoughtful for a moment as they stopped at a red light at the corner of Hermann Drive and Almeda. "Public opinion, I think. You know, people think cops aren't afraid of anything. And that, of course, is just so much hogwash. We're not supermen," he explained, quickly adding, "or women. We're just regular guys with a job to do. Oh, maybe some of us are more concerned with right and wrong than most folks, but by and large, a cop is no different than anyone else. Take me, for instance. I've got a wife and a couple of kids and a house in the suburbs."

The light changed to green and Ben put his foot on the accelerator. "When I go to bed at night, I have the same nightmares as a plumber. When I get up in the morning, I eat the same breakfast as a bus driver. My checkbook balances, or doesn't balance, just like a school teacher's. But because I'm a cop, people expect me to feel differently about things. Sometimes they even stand back a little, waiting to see how I'm going to react. You know, that's why I talked the department into letting me do some public relations work. I like kids. A couple of days a week, I go visit the schools, mostly elementary schools. Sure, there are some trigger-happy cops who give the rest of us a bad name, but they're only a handful—"

Just at that moment, the car radio crackled and sputtered out a call that Wallis could scarcely understand. "That's us," Ben said, reaching for the receiver. Responding quickly to the call, Ben listened carefully to the instructions, translating the shorthand language for Wallis after he spoke some quick words into the receiver. "A car's gone over into the bayou just ahead," he explained, racing toward the scene of the accident. "In this weather, I'm not surprised," he added, gesturing at the scene outside the car window —a gray drizzle that had persisted all evening. "Probably lost control and skidded."

"Is anyone hurt?" Wallis asked, her heart pounding faster at the impending danger. The car was turning down South MacGregor Street, and behind her Wallis could see downtown Houston, the lights of the impressive skyline glistening through the rain.

"Don't know yet," Ben answered, his attention now completely on the road ahead. He had turned on the siren, and the flashing red light on top of the car gave full warning to other vehicles on the street.

Wallis followed his lead, sensing that the time for conversation was over. This was no joyride. She had wanted to experience firsthand some of the real-life problems of being a cop, and she had arranged with Maury Johnson, the chief of police, for a series of Tuesday night forays into the world of law enforcement. On this particular night, as they crossed the Ardmore Street Bridge, there was already a crowd of people gathering, and it wasn't until they had parked the car and gotten out that Wallis saw the dark green sedan nose deep in the bayou. Fortunately, the water level was not very high so that the driver, slouched over the steering wheel, was at least in no danger of drowning.

Quickly assessing the situation, Ben barked out a few sharp commands to the crowd to stand back. Wallis admired the way he took control of the situation, restoring some semblance of order. While Ben radioed for an ambulance, she looked around and realized that if someone didn't start directing traffic, other people might be hurt. Accidents always seemed to attract a large crowd, and this one didn't look any different.

With no thought for her own safety, Wallis grabbed a large flashlight from the floorboard of the patrol car, reached into the back seat for Ben's yellow slicker, and with complete self-assurance made her way through the crowd to the traffic now blocking the bridge. Sure enough, just as she stepped out into the street, she heard a loud crunch and the sound of glass shattering and saw a blue Cadillac rear-end a smaller compact car whose driver had slowed down to see what was happening. Quickly, Wallis stepped into the traffic, stopping one line of cars and motioning another around the broken glass and the two cars now stopped in the middle of the bridge. Still motioning to the moving cars, Wallis hurried along the street, checking both cars to be sure no one was injured.

"Are you all right?" she asked the woman who had been driving the first car. The damage didn't seem to be too bad and, after cautioning two children who were in the back seat to remain there for the time being, Wallis walked around to the second car. The driver was alone and already out of his car, inspecting the minimal damage. When she was satisfied that no one was hurt, Wallis glanced down at the car in the bayou and saw Ben trying to open the car door. He had the help of a couple of bystanders, so Wallis assumed that she was most valuable to him where she was.

Moving quickly back to the center of the street, Wallis calmly continued to direct traffic, listening all the while for the ambulance that would come from the nearby medical center. She knew she had to keep the traffic moving in order to assure the ambulance safe passage to the scene of the accident. She was grateful for the protection of the slicker, realizing that its bright yellow color was clearly visible in the gloomy night. Her long, thick hair was tucked neatly into a French braid that strengthened her authoritative appearance. After all, no one there knew she was wearing an honorary police badge under the slicker. She was glad she'd taken the time to change into comfortable slacks and shoes before meeting Ben at the station house.

After what seemed like an interminable length of time, though she knew it had only been a few short minutes, she heard the shrill siren of the ambulance as it made its way along the other side of the bayou. At almost the same instant, she heard the roar of a rescue helicopter overhead and saw its beacon of light searching the ground below for the wreck. Help was coming all at once.

In a matter of minutes, the ambulance crew had whisked away the injured driver to the nearby medical center, and all that remained of the incident was a couple of wreckers beginning the tedious task of removing the car from the bayou. Two squad cars had also come to the rescue; the officers in them relieved Wallis of her traffic duty and ticketed the drivers of the two cars on the bridge. Ben and Wallis remained at the scene until the green sedan had been towed away. Ben was quite obviously surprised at Wallis's clearheaded response to the emergency, and she knew she had a new friend in the policeman.

Later, as she was driving home from the police station in her own car, she thought back over the evening's events and realized that any doubts she might have had about her plan to get to know the police better had been allayed. She was confident that Ben Chaney would have no qualms about coming to her with future problems or suggestions, and she felt that a door had been opened to better communication.

It was after midnight when Wallis turned the yellow convertible into her own driveway, and she was surprised to see the lights on all over her house. Startled, she hesitated a moment in the driveway, debating whether to proceed any farther. No burglar would turn on all the lights, of that much she was sure, and yet . . . who could it be? As she was deciding what to do, her headlights illuminated a metal shape in the garage, and almost immediately she recognized Sam Davenport's motorcycle.

I might have known, Wallis said to herself with a sigh. Who else in my life turns up so unexpectedly? Not that this should have been unexpected. Sam had been waiting for her every time she'd been out on patrol, but usually on the front porch—not inside the house. She scarcely knew whether to be annoyed or pleased, and she couldn't help wondering how he had gotten into the house.

Parking and locking up the car in the garage, she carefully shut the garage door before heading into the house. She was unaccustomed to having someone waiting at home for her and, in spite of herself, she felt her heart beat a little faster. She liked this man, and she liked being with him.

For three weeks, Sam had been in her thoughts constantly, just beneath the surface no matter what she was doing. The memory of their night together filled her with pleasure, and though they had only seen each other briefly since then, it seemed as though it had happened only yesterday. She had spent some time with him since and found that it was harder and harder to chase that sensual memory from her thoughts. She had a full, complete life without him, and she saw no way to add a romance to her already packed schedule. Romance was not in her scheme of things, but she hadn't counted on meeting someone like Sam. Never had she been so attracted to a man, and suddenly none of the old rules applied. She was definitely breaking new ground.

Nothing, however, had prepared her for the scene she encountered when she walked into the house. At the foot of the stairs were two well-worn and somewhat tattered suitcases! Sniffing the buttery smell of popcorn, Wallis followed the aroma to the kitchen. She had noticed that the video recorder was no longer in its usual place in the living room, and she could hear the muffled sounds of the television set upstairs as she walked into the kitchen, curious to see what had taken place while she was gone. There on the stove were obvious clues—a large sauce pan, a bottle of vegetable oil, half a stick of butter, and two potholders. On the kitchen floor next to the stove sat a pair of brown shoes, and a tan leather jacket hung across the back of one of the kitchen chairs. Sam had made himself right at home, she noted with an amused smile.

I probably should be furious, she thought wryly as she headed up the stairs. It's called breaking and entering, I believe. But she wasn't furious, not a bit. There was something engaging about a man who liked popcorn and old movies as much as she did, and she felt the tensions of the day melt away as she followed the sound of the television set. On the upstairs banister she found a man's turtleneck sweater, which she picked up as she walked by, and on the floor near the bedroom door was one sock. He wasn't the tidiest man in the world, that was for sure. By the time she had followed the trail of shoes and clothes into the bedroom and found Sam propped up in bed with every pillow in the house behind him and a mixing bowl full of popcorn in his lap, Wallis was having a hard time trying not to laugh out loud.

"May I come in?" she asked, peering into the doorway. "I hope I'm not interrupting anything."

"Of course. Do come in," Sam said nonchalantly, putting a handful of popcorn in his mouth. His bare chest was broad and muscular, and his tousled blond hair gave him a boyish appearance that was somehow unexpected in a grown man with a hard-nosed reputation as one of the country's top journalists. "You're just the person I was looking for."

"Well, you've found me," Wallis replied drily, walking across the room. As far as she was concerned, there was nothing predictable about this man. She stood next to the bed and helped herself to some popcorn.

"I don't know," Sam said, looking at her badge doubtfully. "Are you sure this isn't a raid?" His slacks had been tossed across a chair, and it was apparent that he was wearing very little, if anything, under the covers.

Wallis had completely forgotten that she was wearing the badge, and she laughed. "Lucky for you I'm off duty," she said, picking another sock off the floor by the bed. "That's just your guilty conscience working overtime. How did you get in anyway?"

"Now, you know I can't tell you everything. Besides, I might want to do it again sometime," he added with an outrageous grin.

"Is it that easy to get into my house?" Wallis asked, a little disturbed at the thought.

"Well," Sam drawled, relenting, "it is if you can climb a tree and find an unlocked second-story window."

Wallis looked concerned briefly, then laughed. "Well, in any case, I can see you've made yourself quite at home." Holding up the clothes she had gathered along the way, she finished lightheartedly, "Did you have much trouble moving the video recorder up the stairs?"

"I've done easier things in my life," Sam admitted with a boyish grin. How could this be the same man who had won a Pulitzer Prize for his investigative reporting? Contradictions like these were part of what Wallis found so irresistible about him. "But it was well worth the effort, don't you agree?" He moved over and patted the bed beside him, motioning for her to join him.

Unable to make any further protest with a straight face, Wallis tossed the handful of clothes on the chair and sat down on the edge of the bed. When his arms went around her, she let herself be pulled close. Her hands caught at the tangle of hair on his chest, her lips pressed against his in a delicious kiss, his salty tongue teased the softness of her mouth. Wallis was amazed at how natural it seemed, having this man in her bed holding her in his arms, and she was lost in the magic of it, helpless against the tumultuous clamor of her own feelings.

Pushing away ever so slightly, her lips still grazing his, she asked, her soft voice a little husky, "Do you plan to stay long?" She was thinking of the two large suitcases at the foot of the stairs.

"As long as you'll let me," Sam answered, his blue eyes searching hers, looking for the words his lips wouldn't let her say. It was clear no further answer was needed, and as his lips again pressed hard against hers, he ran his hand through her thick soft hair, his fingers loosening the twists of the French braid until the long, silky tendrils were free and falling onto her shoulders.

"In that case, I think I'd better slip into something

a little less formal, don't you think?" As she spoke, her lips and tongue tickled the outer edge of his ear and her hands moved playfully across his chest.

"Now you're talking," Sam agreed, giving her one last hug. "That badge is a little unsettling, I have to admit. You know, I was just beginning to like you as a mayor. This new role will take some getting used to."

Wallis grinned, giving him one last kiss before she worked herself free of his arms and stood up. "What's the matter? Don't you think you can handle the officer behind the badge?" She was pulling her shirttails from the tailored trousers.

"Handling you is just exactly what I had in mind," Sam answered, making a grab at her and attempting to pull her back down. "Here, let me help you."

"Oh no, you don't," she laughed, heading for the bathroom. "Believe it or not, I've still got a few things to do before I fall into bed with you. I just walked in the door, remember?" She was suddenly beginning to feel the need to be alone for a few minutes, to gather her thoughts and her presence of mind. Being with Sam always brought on a flood of emotions, and she didn't like being overwhelmed—not by him, not by anyone. It wasn't that she didn't like what was happening. It was just that she had had a long, hard day. A bath would feel good.

"That's not something I'm likely to forget any time soon," Sam said, falling back against the pillows with a sigh. He switched on the television again, prepared to wait. "Hey, how does this movie end, anyway?"

Wallis shut the bathroom door behind her and started her bath water. She stuck her head back out the door. "You mean this is the first time you've seen *The African Queen?*" She was truly amazed, and her wide amber eyes reflected her astonishment.

"Of course I've seen it," Sam said, not without some indignation. He stuffed some more popcorn into his mouth. "I just don't remember how it ends."

Wallis walked back into the bedroom wearing only her shirt, revealing long, shapely legs. As she spoke she unbuttoned her shirt. "Oh, sure you do. The Germans have the river sealed off. Charlie wants to wait out the war but she insists they go on down river." By this time, Wallis was sitting on the bed again, watching the movie and eating popcorn.

"He gets drunk and she throws his gin bottles overboard, right?" Sam ran his finger gently across her cheek, pushing her hair from her face.

"You *have* seen it," Wallis said, looking at him accusingly. She was so completely caught up in their conversation that she had forgotten her bathwater.

Sam pulled her close and kissed her on the mouth, his hands unfastening the last button on her shirt. "Of course. I told you that," he said, between kisses. "But what happens to the *African Queen?*"

"Hey, why did you move the video recorder upstairs anyway? If you're going to ask me to tell you the whole story you could have saved yourself the trouble." Wallis put her arms around his neck.

"So I could get you in bed with me," Sam explained patiently, his lips claiming hers once again.

"You haven't had much difficulty so far," Wallis whispered in his ear.

"Just didn't want to take any chances," Sam answered, opening her shirt and tenderly cupping her ample breasts.

Wallis moaned with pleasure, her back arching slightly against the pressure of his hands, her lips parting eagerly as his tongue sought out the velvet secrets of her mouth. She gave herself over to the moment. Nothing else mattered. When Sam leaned back against the pillows, pulling her down alongside him, she playfully acquiesced, her hands tangled in his hair, her lips and tongue teasing his ear.

"It sinks, you know," she said, apropos of nothing.

Sam stopped kissing her, a quizzical look on his face. "Sinks?"

"The *African Queen*," Wallis elaborated, biting his shoulder gently.

"No, it doesn't," Sam said emphatically, giving her nose a pinch. "That's the German ship."

"No, no, no. The *African Queen* sinks first. The Germans get theirs later." Wallis snuggled deeper into Sam's arms, luxuriating in the warmth of his embrace and running her foot across his leg, her toes tickling him seductively.

"Which reminds me," Sam said. "You probably have enough water in there to sink two ships, don't you think?"

"Oh, no! The bathwater!" Wallis sat bolt upright, aghast. Leaping to her feet, she made a mad dash for the bathroom just in time to turn off the water before the tub overflowed. "Don't go away," she called over her shoulder as she shut the bathroom door behind her.

"Don't worry," Sam said with a grin. "I'm here to stay."

The bubble bath Wallis had poured in had foamed wonderfully, and as she slipped out of her clothes and into the water, she enjoyed the sweet aroma of the soothing bubbles. Soaking for just a few minutes in the hot tub, she wondered briefly what Sam had meant by that last remark, but it was only a passing thought. For the first time in her life, she was content to let things happen without a plan.

Stepping out of the bathtub a few minutes later, Wallis reflected on the unexpected twists life sometimes takes. Who would have thought a month ago that she, Mayor Wallis Carmichael, would fall in love with a man, and a reporter at that? For so many years she had been so intent on her career that she had truly given very little thought to her personal life.

After drying off, Wallis reached for the full-length white terry-cloth robe that hung on the bathroom door. After belting the robe at the waist, she brushed her long hair vigorously for a few minutes. A moment or two by herself was all she really needed, and when she joined Sam in the bedroom, she was ready to pick up where they'd left off. The soothing effects of the bath had washed away any second thoughts she might have had about the wisdom of this relationship, with its chance meetings and lack of conventional restraints.

"Hi, gorgeous," Sam said with a low whistle as she walked across the bedroom to the bed. "You were right. It did sink."

"Did you doubt me?" Wallis said with a little pout, pretending to be hurt. She sat down on the bed beside him.

"Not for a moment," Sam said, putting his arms around her and pulling her close, his lips meeting hers hungrily.

As if the few minutes that had separated them were all that was needed to fuel the fire, their embrace was even more intense than before, and when Sam reached over to turn off the television, Wallis didn't object. The sudden silence of the room enveloped them like the softness of a down comforter, shielding them from the outside world. They were lovers, alone at last.

As Sam lay back on the bed and pulled her over on top of him, so that the full weight of her body stretched across his, Wallis felt a rush of desire sweep through her slender frame, and roughly pulling his thick tousled hair, she took the initiative, pushing her tongue eagerly between his parted lips. His hands moved from her shoulders up and down her back, holding her thighs against his hard maleness, his hips moving rhythmically beneath her. Wallis felt herself stiffen, sweet agony filling her body with thrills of pleasure.

"I like holding you in my arms," he whispered, his warm breath soft against her ear.

"And I like you to hold me in your arms," Wallis

said, raising herself on her elbows. The soft terry-cloth robe fell open, revealing her star-white flesh.

"Oh, God," Sam moaned, his hands moving to cup her pear-shaped breasts, "you're so beautiful."

Wallis leaned forward slightly, eloquently answering him with her body instead of words, guiding one breast to his mouth, her hands still caught in his hair. The sweet sensation of his mouth and tongue on her sensitive flesh was all that she'd hoped it would be, and she moved her torso back and forth slowly, teasing his mouth with first one nipple and then the other. His mouth and tongue and fingers sought her breasts eagerly until the large brown nipples were hard with desire, and Wallis, sensing the powerful strength of his need beneath her, arched her slender form, her head thrown back, her long thick hair falling freely about her shoulders.

"Oh, Sam," she moaned hoarsely, her body taut with desire, "you are so good to me." And unable to stand the exquisite torture even a moment longer, she rolled over on her back, pulling him over with her.

Suspended above her, Sam looked down into her face, his blue eyes glazed over with a passion so great he could scarcely speak. "No, my love. It's the other way around." With that, he pushed up one arm and with his free hand, loosened the robe that was still between them, revealing her nakedness to his admiring eyes. Deftly he pulled off the robe, his trailing hand following his eyes across her aroused and trembling body.

Wallis moved rhymthically beneath his touch, her breasts taut, the full nipples hard. As if inviting him to take her, Wallis opened her legs slightly, her hips undulating gracefully. Sam understood the unspoken message, and his hands and mouth obeyed without question, moving down her body searching for new ways to excite her. This time his touch was even more sensitive than it had been that first night. He seemed to know intuitively what she wanted and how to give it to her with infinite patience, and Wallis responded with every ounce of her being, giving herself to him completely.

With masterful skill, Sam brought her to the brink of ecstasy, and sensing that the tension was right, he brought his face up to hers, his blue eyes filled with smoldering desire, as if to verify with his intellect what his emotions and his body had already told him. He found the fire in her amber eyes, the sign he was looking for, and raising his body over hers, he entered her, his body leading hers in the timeless rhythms, urging her on to greater and greater heights of erotic pleasure until finally, finally, she reached the top, the moment of completion, and there was nothing else. The moment was marked by her soft moan of joy, breaking the silence, the spell that bound them. With perfect timing, Sam followed her lead and a few moments later, he answered with a shuddering gasp of his own. The ride down was a gentle one for them both as they lay locked in each other's arms, a moist tangle of exhausted lovers.

A few moments later, Sam sat up and looked at

Wallis. "What do you say we watch the end of *The African Queen* tomorrow night?"

"Mmmm," was Wallis's response. "That's *another* great idea," she whispered, as if tomorrow night, and the night after that, and the one after that were all his to do with as he chose.

6

Hey, good-lookin','' Sam's deep voice drawled behind Wallis, and a warm hand slid down her shoulder, making its way through the silky folds of her pale pink shirt. Wallis gasped a little when his fingers touched her breast and his lips nuzzled her neck.

"Talking to me?" Wallis asked, giving in to the urge to tease him. She closed the book and reached up to touch his face. She was stretched out on the white chaise lounge in her bedroom, trying to read a murder mystery, but it wasn't holding her interest. When she had come home that evening, Sam had insisted that she get off her feet and relax for a few minutes while he finished preparing supper. She had been grateful for his thoughtful consideration. As he

knew, her day had been complicated and she needed a chance to unwind. The confirmation of Patten
Roberts by the City Council had been the highlight
of the morning, but the moment of triumph had
been short-lived.

Immediately after the break for lunch, Ivy had
brought her the first reports on the Gulf Coast
Development Corporation. Wallis had a chance only
to glance through it, but even upon a cursory reading
it was troubling. The city contract for the new
monorail system had been awarded some months
earlier, before the former director had resigned to
take a job in a city less beleaguered by transit
problems. Unless the plan for a monorail system was
scrapped, Gulf Coast Development Corporation
would be the company to build it. And Patten
Roberts had made no secret of his enthusiastic
support of the idea.

"Sure looks that way." Sam answered, interrupting her thoughts as he sat down on the edge of the
chaise lounge and kissed her gently on the lips, his
hands holding her face up to meet his.

Wallis put her arms around his neck, determined
to push aside the worries of the day. "What do you
say we talk some more?"

Sam's strong hands encircled her slender waist,
and his blue eyes twinkled. He knew she was making
an effort to be lighthearted. "You're reading my
mind," he said teasingly between kisses.

"Of course," Wallis whispered as her fingers
trailed across his shoulder. "I'm clairvoyant." She

leaned back in the long, comfortable chair, relaxed, the tribulations of the day almost forgotten as Sam playfully showered her with kisses.

"In that case, what am I thinking now?" he retorted with good humor. His hands toyed seductively with the buttons on her silk shirt as he stopped kissing Wallis and assumed a thoughtful expression for a moment.

She answered his challenge with a grin. "Oh, that's easy. But it's X-rated, not something I'd repeat in mixed company."

Sam threw back his head and roared with laughter.

"Now that's a cop-out if I've ever heard one— though come to think of it, you're right." While he was talking, Sam had mastered the buttons on her shirt and had pulled her close to him, his cheek against the sensitive flesh of her exposed breast.

"This is one sure way to get my mind off my work," Wallis whispered softly, kissing his ear and pulling his hair gently.

"There's nothing I'd like better than to make you forget the rest of the world." Sam kissed the firm rounded flesh of her breast.

"You're not doing such a bad job of it right now," Wallis said, her voice husky.

Reluctantly, Sam pulled away. "But it's only a momentary diversion, I'm afraid," he said with resignation. "Supper's almost ready, and I'm not about to ruin it now, not after I've been slaving over a hot stove all afternoon."

Wallis was properly chastened. "I haven't been much help, have I?"

"That's okay," Sam assured her with a smile, as he buttoned her blouse. "Next time I'm up against a deadline, you can do the honors."

"You've got a deal," Wallis promised. Then she added thoughtfully, "Did you get any writing done today?"

"About ten pages," Sam answered. "I like to write and cook at the same time—one thing sort of feeds into the other." He poked at her playfully as he stood up. "That's why you're going to have such a fine meal tonight. Now you'd better hurry up. It's almost ready."

"Give me half a minute and I'll be down." Wallis looked up at him with real affection, watching him as he left the room. She couldn't help laughing to herself as she heard him taking the stairs two at a time. He was truly a special man.

Leaving her book open on the chaise lounge, Wallis got up and walked across the room to her dresser. She studied her reflection in the mirror, thinking about her life these past few weeks since Sam had moved in. Certainly her life had changed for the better. She would never have thought it possible to be as busy as she was—and every day the office she held grew more demanding—and still have time enough for a romance. And romantic it was, there was no denying that. Wallis had never enjoyed such a frankly sexual relationship. There had been other men in her life, of course. She was no innocent child being swept off her feet. But no one had made her feel the way Sam did, had ever touched her so deeply.

There was more to this relationship than mere sexual attraction. They enjoyed each other's company and never ran out of things to say, things to share with each other. Sam's schedule was considerably more flexible than hers, and almost before Wallis realized it, they were sharing all the household chores. He had woven himself so swiftly and easily into the fabric of her life that she almost could not remember a time when they hadn't been together. Some nights she cooked supper. Some nights he took over by himself. The best nights, of course, were those when they cooked together, trying out new recipes, each learning something from the other. Sometimes they went out for a hot dog and took in a movie. She wondered how she had ever managed to get along without him.

The joys of domesticity were not the only ones they shared. Since Sam was still covering the City Hall beat for one of the papers, she saw him nearly every day, and at night she looked forward to reading his perceptive comments on the political life of the city. She was learning a lot from Sam, both from the man and from his writing. He had been writing a lot. He was excited about the novel he was working on and seemed pleased with the results so far, though he was more reticent about sharing this new venture with her than he was with his shorter articles. She understood that it was an ambitious undertaking for him—fiction was so different from the investigative reporting that had made him famous—and she respected his need for privacy. He had staked out an office for himself in the guest room, and nearly every night as she was falling asleep, Wallis was conscious of the distant sound of the typewriter, telling her he was hard at work. It was a comfortable sound and made her feel complete in a way she never had before.

Being in love, that's what it is. Being in love. With this thought, Wallis shook herself free of her reverie, brought herself back to the present, and gave her long, thick curls a few vigorous strokes before deciding that a touch of lipstick was in order. The few minutes of repose had restored her sense of order and she could look back over the day with considerably more equanimity than had been possible earlier. She knew she was facing real trouble ahead with the Gulf Coast Development Corporation and the monorail contract, but she had no doubts about her ability to do what was necessary.

"Hey, come on down, Sleeping Beauty. Supper's ready," Sam's cheerful voice called up the stairs.

Taking her cue, Wallis headed down the stairs. "All right already, I'm coming," she said, laughing. By the time she got to the kitchen, Sam was carrying a casserole dish to the table, and the pungent aroma of garlic, butter, and onions filled the room.

"Mmmm. Smells delicious. What is it?" Wallis picked up the water glasses sitting on the counter and took them to the table that Sam had already set.

"Something special I whipped up for the occasion —my mother's chicken spaghetti." With a little flourish, Sam lit the two candles in the center of the table.

"The occasion?" Wallis was puzzled for a minute.

"Yes, the occasion—or have you already forgotten that your first political appointment was confirmed today?" Sam sat down across from Wallis. "That was, by the way, an admirable display of support. Why don't we drink to that?" He picked up his wine glass and toasted her.

"Thank you," Wallis said, looking a bit sheepish. "But to tell you the truth, I had almost forgotten about Patten Roberts." With as little fanfare as possible, she told him about Gulf Coast Development Corporation's current contract with the city. When she was finished, she waited for his reaction.

Sam was silent. Instead of replying, he began to serve the food. Wallis took the full plate he handed her. She guessed that he was politely refraining from saying, "I told you so." She was grateful for his tact and didn't mind saying so.

"Thanks, Sam—" she began.

"Oh, it's my pleasure." Sam didn't let her finish. He was filling his plate with chicken spaghetti. "It's a secret recipe I stole from my mother."

"No, no. Not the supper, though thanks are certainly in order there too." Wallis took a bite of her meal. "But I mean to thank you for not saying I told you so."

"Oh, you mean the monorail business," Sam said nonchalantly, spreading his napkin on his lap.

"Yes, I mean the monorail business," Wallis said a

bit peevishly, mimicking his unconcern. "And you know that's what I mean."

"Yeah, I know. I'm sorry. It's just that I'm worried. Really worried. Someone's in this up to his—or her—ears. Someone who understands city contracts. Someone with access to permits and city inspectors." Sam reached across the table and patted her arm gently. "But you've got other things to think about. I don't want to worry you with my suspicions." There was a frown on his face.

"Now, Sam, don't tell me I shouldn't worry my pretty little head. I feel that there's something you're not telling me." Wallis stopped her fork in midair. "I'm mayor of this city and I need to know." Wallis looked across at him steadily for a moment, searching his face. "There *is* something you're not telling me, isn't there?"

"No, no, of course not." Sam was almost too quick with his denial. He had gotten up to get the wine and was pouring a second glass for Wallis.

"I'd like to believe you. I really would," she said animatedly. She was buttering a piece of French bread, and her cheeks were flushed.

"Listen," Sam said, "all I've got right now are some hunches. The minute I've got any hard facts, you'll be the first to know." He covered her hand with his. "I promise." His soft voice was compelling.

"Okay," Wallis sighed as she set down her glass. "But I don't like it. I don't like it one bit," she commented, more to herself than to Sam.

Sam eyed her thoughtfully before he replied. "What you need, my friend, is something to get your mind off your work, and I have just the thing." Sam had started clearing away the table.

"Oh, you do, do you?" Wallis said with a laugh as she pushed back her chair.

"Just what the doctor ordered." Sam had a mysterious smile on his face.

"Well, are you going to tell me, or do I have to guess?" Wallis started stacking the dishes in the dishwasher.

"Guess what's on at the River Oaks Theater tonight? You've got three chances." Sam was not to be hurried.

"Gone with the Wind?" Wallis tried, falling into the spirit of things.

"Oh, come on, Wally," Sam said indignantly. "Would I get all worked up about wilted magnolias and Clark Gable?" Sam had a pained expression on his face.

Wallis laughed. "No, I guess not. It's really something special, isn't it?" She stopped what she was doing and gave every impression of thinking very hard.

"Of course, it's special. This is still a celebration, isn't it?" Sam had his back to Wallis as he turned on the water in the sink and began rinsing the pans.

"I don't think you're going to let it be anything but a celebration," Wallis conceded with a laugh. She put her hands on her hips and looked up, as if the answer was written on the ceiling. She bit her lip.

When she had been silent for a few moments, Sam said a trifle impatiently, "Hey, you're not giving up already, are you?" He turned around to face her, drying off the heavy skillet with a dishcloth.

"Of course not. I'm trying to read your mind, which is a little difficult with the water running."

"Oh, if that's your only problem . . ." Sam quickly turned off the water. "Now you—"

"Shhhhh," Wallis warned, putting a finger to her lips. "It's coming. Now I'm getting . . ."

"Boy, what an act!" Sam said, interrupting. "You know, Wally, maybe you should take this clairvoyance of yours seriously. I mean, you could resign as mayor—"

Wallis turned to him and said, "It's Hepburn and Tracy, isn't it?"

Sam looked taken aback. He folded his arms across his chest, crossed his feet, and leaned back against the counter. "Go on."

"I thought so," Wallis said, triumphantly. She turned and started out of the kitchen, her hands behind her back, pacing as she thought.

"That could just be a lucky guess," Sam said, a bit petulantly. "Hepburn and Tracy made a lot of movies. You've still got two guesses."

Wallis turned just as she got to the door and started walking around the kitchen. "I don't need two more guesses." She was being theatrical and she knew it.

"Okay?" Sam waited, his face skeptical.

"Desk Set," Wallis said, grinning.

Sam was crestfallen. "How did you know?"

"I told you. I read your mind." Wallis was laughing. "I also read the paper this morning and saw the ad."

"What a sneak," Sam said with feigned disgust. "And to think I was trying to cheer you up." He started the water in the sink again.

"Does that mean you're not going to take me?" Wallis walked up behind him and put her arms around his waist, giving him a conciliatory hug.

Sam turned off the water and turned around to face her, his hands at her waist. "If you promise not to start that clairvoyant stuff again. You know, for a minute you had me really thinking you could read my mind. And that's a little unsettling." He kissed her gently on the lips.

"It's a promise," Wallis said, giving him a return kiss on the lips. "What time's the show?"

"Any minute now. We'd better hurry," Sam said, wiping off the counter one more time.

"Great, but I want to change into something more comfortable before we leave." Wallis pushed the chairs under the table and dashed upstairs to change clothes.

She dressed hurriedly, looking forward to the movie and the time with Sam. Usually she worried about appearing in public informally, but tonight she didn't give it a thought. Even the mayor had a right to a private life, and this evening was going to be all hers. Combing through her closet, she quickly selected a pair of tailored but comfortable trousers, donned a crisp yellow oxford shirt, and tied a tailored cardigan around her shoulders. Quickly brushing her hair back, she grabbed her leather purse and bound-ed down the steps. Sam was waiting for her at the front door, anxiously checking his watch.

"We're going to have to hurry," he said a bit crossly. "That's the trouble with surprise celebrations —they're so hard to schedule."

Wallis made a little face. "Then next time don't surprise me." She took his arm and they went out the door. Sam led her down the sidewalk to where his motorcycle was parked, and Wallis stopped dead in her tracks. "Oh, no, you don't. I'm not going anywhere on that thing. We can take my car."

Sam more or less ignored her and put on his helmet. He looked up at her, the expression on his face unreadable behind the tinted shield, but his voice was as teasing as ever. "You don't mean to tell me that Ms. Mayor is afraid to ride a motorcycle?"

"Not afraid," Wallis insisted. "It's just that I don't want my hair to get blown around."

"Sure, sure," Sam taunted. "Feminine vanity. I know the type. Come on, Wallis," he added in a pleading tone, "you've never even tried it. I'll go slowly and I think you'll like it, I really do. It's a lot of fun once you get used to it."

"Well, all right," Wallis conceded and began strapping on the helmet Sam held out to her. She hated to admit it, but more than once she had wondered what it would be like to go speeding along on the big machine with Sam. However, now that the opportunity had presented itself, she wasn't sure about it. She took a seat behind him and wrapped her arms securely around his lean form. "I'm ready. Let's take off."

Sam gave her a mischievous grin, the white of his teeth just visible below the visor, and the powerful machine sprang into life. True to his word, Sam did take it slowly, and Wallis found that the experience was quite exhilerating. Her hair was securely tucked beneath the helmet, and she enjoyed the sensation of the landscape rushing by, the feel of the cool night air against her face. When they stopped at the corner, Sam turned to see the expression on her face. "All right?" he asked. Her glowing face gave him the answer. Wallis loved it—she had never felt so free in her life.

The drive to the nearby River Oaks Theater went by all too quickly for Wallis's taste, and she was genuinely sorry when it was over, though she was looking forward to the movie. She and Sam took their places in the ticket line, helmets under their arms, and if anyone recognized Wallis in the short line, she was grateful that they didn't make an issue of it.

That was one of the few things about being in politics that Wallis hadn't quite gotten used to, even after all these years. Her private life was always subject to scrutiny, and though she'd never done anything she wouldn't want anyone to know about, she often was uncomfortable being the focus of so much attention. But tonight she didn't really care. She enjoyed being with Sam so much that she didn't mind if people saw them together. Not that she'd want it all over the papers that they were living together, of course. Living together. Wallis ran the words over in her mind. They had a nice sound, she thought. Looking up at Sam, who was buying the tickets, she felt a thrill of pride rush through her, and she realized that this relationship gave her as much pleasure as her career did. What a first! Wallis thought to herself.

Sam took her arm companionably as they entered the theater and gave their tickets to the doorman. Sam directed her to the refreshment stand and stood looking down at her with an amused grin. "Well, lady, what'll it be?" He gestured at the counter.

Wallis grinned up at him mischievously. "I think I'll settle for all the comforts of home. Popcorn with lots of butter and a soft drink, please. And maybe some chocolate-covered almonds, too." She watched the grin on his face turn to an expression of mock horror. "You can't be that hungry. Either you really aren't or you lied about liking my chicken spaghetti." Leaning down to whisper in her ear, he added, "And don't tease about all the comforts of home or I'll take you back there. You realize, of course, that if we were at home, we'd at least be watching the movie from the comfort of a large bed."

Wallis blushed—partly with pleasure, partly from the teasing. "But I don't have this movie on tape," she teased him in return.

Sam turned to purchase their refreshments and spoke through gritted teeth. "Next time, I'll arrange it. I'm not so sure I like taking you out like this. Too many envious glances."

Wallis reached over to carry her share of the refreshments and led Sam up the stairs to the balcony. "I see you've been here before," he said to her. "Or is heading for the balcony just an impulse left over from junior high school?"

"I've been here before," she returned, laughing. "As a matter of fact, it's one of the few places I see as often as my house or my office." And it was true. Whenever she felt she had the time, she took in one of the River Oaks' movies, and the balcony seemed completely secluded. It was one of her few private pleasures and she was delighted that it was a pastime that Sam wanted to share with her.

As the lights went down and Sam's arm crept around her shoulders, Wallis snuggled down into her seat and prepared to enjoy the evening's outing, all thoughts of the problems of the day temporarily disappearing. She munched her popcorn happily, conscious of Sam's presence next to her in the dark, and a thrill of anticipation ran through her—partly the usual feeling she had at the beginning of a movie, partly the result of thinking ahead toward the close of the evening, when she and Sam would be alone together again.

They watched the movie in total silence, as devoted moviegoers do, and Wallis found that she was soon caught up in the antics of Hepburn and Tracy, admiring, as she always did, their cool wit and intelligence. She laughed at Tracy's portrayal of an efficiency expert and admired Hepburn in her role as research librarian. Sam and I are a lot like them, she thought to herself. We disagree a lot, and we fight a lot, but we do love each other. She felt a tingle of warmth at the knowledge, and denying all the instincts that told her not to do it, she leaned to her left and tugged at Sam's sleeve for attention. "I love you, Sam," she whispered, when he leaned down to see what she wanted.

"I love you too, Wallis," he whispered back, his lips gently grazing the curve of her ear. They both settled back in their seats to watch the movie, but it was as if some subtle current of energy lay between them for the next hour.

When the movie was over and the lights came back on again, Wallis looked up almost shyly to see Sam grinning down at her with a look of tenderness in his eyes. They stood up and made their way through the crowd, down the stairs to the lobby and out into the cool night. Standing there on the sidewalk, Sam gestured at a small restaurant across the street. "Want to have a drink—or some dessert, maybe?"

Wallis's attention was temporarily distracted by someone who asked for her autograph. She hastily signed a scrap of paper and turned back to face him. "No," she said with a wide smile. "After all that popcorn, I don't think I could hold another thing. Besides, I find myself longing for the comforts of home again."

"There you go—reading my mind again," Sam said agreeably. "Let's head for the comforts of home."

They headed around the side of the theater to the parking lot, holding hands, both of them swinging helmets from their free hands. As they reached the motorcycle, they quickly strapped on their helmets and Wallis took her place behind him. She leaned forward and clasped her arms around his waist, pulling him close. "And Sam," she said in a conspiratorial tone, "I think I could get used to this motorcycle. It's a lot of fun. So I don't think you need to take it easy going home. In fact, I think you'd better hurry."

And that's exactly what he did.

7

Wallis rolled over in bed, pushing her hair out of her eyes, and studied Sam's sleeping form with pleasure, a pleasure intensified by her memories of the night before. His blond hair was tousled and he seemed to be at peace, his breathing deep and even. She wanted to reach out and touch him, but she was afraid of waking him. There was no point in getting him up just because she had to go to the office.

She looked at the clock, and a worried frown crossed her face. Later than usual, she thought. I'm going to have to hurry. She slipped quietly from the bed, reaching for her bathrobe and wrapping its warm length around her as she headed for the shower on tiptoe. If only she didn't wake Sam.

The steamy shower brought Wallis back to life,

and soon her thoughts turned to the office, to the difficult day ahead. Patten was going to make his first official presentation to council for the transit system. The new monorail—important as it was—was only part of the plan. New buses, expansion of routes, contraflow lanes on all major freeways, and a computerized system of van sharing were all part of the package. She was pleased with most of it but knew there would be some strong opposition. The contraflow lanes were highly controversial, as was the monorail. But all the pieces would fall into place; she was sure of it, even though there would have to be some compromises along the way.

No, what was really troubling her was the city contract for the monorail. She had set up a meeting with the city attorneys for that afternoon after the council session. Some action would have to be taken, and the sooner the better. What would happen to the monorail was the big question in her mind. The Gulf Coast Development Corporation simply couldn't be the one to build it. She hated to see Patten's plans linked in any way to the scandal, but at the moment she didn't see a way around it.

The evening out with Sam had been a welcome respite from all this. But that was over and it was time to get back to work. She was glad to see that she was as clearheaded as ever. Being in love had made all the difference in her life, and it was with pleasure that she looked back at the night before. She was so lost in her thoughts that she was surprised to realize that she wasn't alone in the shower.

"Hmmmm, looks serious," a low voice said, startling her. She tilted her head back to rinse shampoo out of her hair and turned to face Sam.

"Where did you come from?" she demanded. "Are you sneaking around or something?"

"Now see here," he answered, "I made plenty of noise getting out of bed and coming in here and brushing my teeth. You were so lost in thought that you didn't hear. Besides, as the new tenant, I thought it was my duty to help you conserve water, so here I am." And without another word, he reached for the soap, working up a froth of scented lather with his hands. Then he reached for Wallis, his hands covering her breasts with bubbles. She trembled at his touch, responding to his teasing all too quickly.

"Come on, Sam," Wallis pleaded, knowing that this could lead to only one thing—not that she minded, but it was late and she wanted to be at the office by eight.

"All right." He smiled agreeably, reaching for her now soapy body and pulling her against him. "I hate to rush these things, but if you're in a hurry, I'll do my best to oblige."

Wallis couldn't help but laugh. She should have known he'd have an answer for anything she could come up with. That was part of his charm—he wasn't the least bit intimidated by her. She leaned against him—only for a moment, she promised herself—enjoying the texture of his soapy chest against her breasts, the stinging needles of the shower spray, the warmth of his body next to hers. No matter what he did, the man was irresistible.

She stepped back, trying to rinse some of the soap bubbles from her body under the spray of water, but Sam wasn't about to let her go so easily. His fingers teased the delicate flesh of her breasts, tracing lazy, soapy circles across her skin. He touched each nipple in turn, gently arousing her.

"Now, Sam," she said, "you know I have a busy day today, and this just isn't the time." She hoped her voice sounded firm, for her body was melting under his touch.

"Oh, yes, it is," he answered, his voice full of sensual persuasion, murmuring huskily as he leaned forward to claim her mouth in a good-morning kiss. "This is the perfect time. Maybe not the right place, but the perfect time." And then his lips silenced her protest. Wallis knew that she was lost as she surrendered to his kiss, her arms slowly sliding upward to encircle his neck as she pressed her body against his, returning the warmth and pressure of his mouth.

Wallis let her tongue search him out, teasing him, enjoying this love play in the shower. It seemed that the world they inhabited was all warmth and steam and moisture, and she could feel the muscles in her body relax into a sensual languor. She inhaled the fragrance of the soap, the scent of Sam's body, and she deepened the kiss, pleased at his response.

"You know," he muttered softly, his lips teasing her neck, "we are wasting time. It would be a lot easier if we were more comfortable."

Wallis grinned. "I don't know about you, but I'm perfectly comfortable. I thought you had an adventurous nature." Her arms still around his neck, she drew back, her eyes half-closed with pleasure, and surveyed him from beneath her lashes, waiting to see what he would do next.

"I always think it's best to stick with the tried and true, especially in the morning," he said, laughing, "but . . . I'm flexible." And as if to prove it, he held her gently, moving against her, with her, in her, seeming to have only her pleasure in mind, until it seemed that she could hardly stand it. The warm spray of the shower cascaded over them, and Wallis felt that she had never been surrounded by such a sensual atmosphere. She also realized with a start that she had never been so unselfconscious. She chuckled, realizing how unlikely she once would have thought this whole experience. Sam gave her a questioning look, and pulling her close, reminded her quite firmly of where she was and what they were doing.

"I'm glad to see you're enjoying this," he murmured, "but I didn't mean to be funny."

Wallis clung to him, her sole support in this moment of warmth and moisture. "Oh, it's not funny," she assured him. "It's that it's so wonderful."

Reassured, Sam continued to move her against him, teasing her, tormenting her, until with a shudder of pleasure she began to move herself, his arms supporting her as she moved up and down, finally letting out a sigh of ecstasy and exhaustion as they reached the peak. Slowly, slowly, Sam lifted her up slightly, then lowered her to stand against him, their bodies pressed against each other tenderly, as if the passion that had only moments before possessed them had been no substitute for the simple pleasure of being held and touched.

Still the water cascaded around them. Wallis lifted her face to his, tears of joy mingling with the spray of the shower. She gently brushed his lips with hers, thanking him silently. Her wet hair streamed down her back as she stood there for a moment, looking at him.

Sam gave her a tender smile, his eyes searching her face. A mischievous grin broke the spell as he spoke. "I like this," he said teasingly. "At least I don't have to worry about your attention straying to the nearest clock."

"The time!" Wallis gasped. All thoughts of the day had been driven from her mind by their interlude of shared pleasure. But now she was firmly back in the real world. The water of the shower, as if to reinforce that reality, was now tepid. "I'm going to be late—I just know it." She scrambled out of the shower, reaching for the nearest available towel and mumbling as she went. "And today of all days. Sam, you know I hate to be late. And you deliberately . . ."

She looked up to see a satisfied grin on his face and they both began laughing together. "Oh, well," she conceded, "I guess this once it won't matter. But really—" She wrapped the towel around her as she reached for her hair dryer. In only a few short minutes she had dried her hair and restored it to its usual gleaming order. Racing into the bedroom, she hurriedly dressed in one of her favorite outfits—a slim black gabardine suit, its severely tailored lines softened by a white silk shirt and a maroon silk bow tie. Giving Sam a quick good-bye kiss, she dashed down the stairs and out the door.

Wallis was humming to herself as she walked into the outer office. Sam had been right. It was a good way to start the day. But one look at Ivy's face brought her up short. "What's the matter?" she asked, prepared for the worst. She hadn't even had a chance to put her purse down and she was already faced with the latest crisis.

"I'm glad you're in a good mood," Ivy said testily, ruffling her blond hair with impatient fingers. "You're going to need every bit of good humor you can muster to handle all the bad news I've got this morning. Haven't you seen the morning paper?"

"Not yet," Wallis admitted, embarrassed. "I overslept." That was close enough to the truth, she decided.

"It's just as well," Ivy continued. "Take a look at this." And she passed the front page over to Wallis.

"Dayton Says Monorail Is Waste of Taxpayers' Money," read the headline, and Wallis groaned in despair as she read the accompanying news story. Patten Roberts had scarcely been confirmed and Ernie was already out for blood. Roberts' folly he was calling the system, describing the architectural design as unsafe and unworkable. Someone had to warn the public, Dayton was quoted as saying. As much as she hated to, Wallis had to admit, "Ernie's got clout, there's no doubt about it. We're going to hear about this."

"We already are. The phone's been ringing off the

wall," Ivy told her. "But I didn't start answering it until eight o'clock."

"He's trying to get at me, you know, through Patten." Wallis was talking as much to herself as she was to Ivy. "And the terrible thing about it is that the city will suffer in the long run. I think this monorail is really what we need." She paused thoughtfully, twisting the paper in her hands. "I wonder how much damage Ernie can really do."

"Patten has scheduled a press conference at four this afternoon, but I'm afraid that won't keep the reporters away from you in the meantime." There was concern in Ivy's voice.

"I can deal with that," Wallis said absently. "What worries me is the contract. That whole thing is about to go up in smoke and when it does, we may not be able to save the monorail. There's already enough doubt as it is. One more problem may be the last straw. And Patten's going to be held responsible for it, just by association. It's not going to make his job any easier."

"Leave it to Ernie to make things more complicated," Ivy concurred. "The evidence is sure stacking up against the Gulf Coast Development Corporation, isn't it?"

"Yes, it is. The city attorneys are about to move. Ernie's timing couldn't have been worse." There was real bitterness in her voice. Wallis shook her head doubtfully. "You know, I think Sam's right. All the evidence points to *someone* with authority, someone within the system. I'm afraid this is all bigger than it looks on paper."

"Now don't go looking for trouble," Ivy warned, her face a study in determination. "You know, Wallis, Patten's strong enough to withstand this. He knew he was taking on a lot when he took the job. You've got to give him more credit. Don't let this thing get the best of you. It's not our only worry." Ivy paused a minute before she went on. "This newspaper story is the first thing I wanted to tell you about this morning. The second might be even more serious. Rumor has it that the contract negotiations with the sanitation workers aren't going well at all. We could have a strike on our hands."

"That's all we need," Wallis said with feeling. "Why does everything have to fall apart at once?" She tugged at her silk bow tie.

"Oh, Wallis," Ivy laughed. "That's the way it always is in politics. You know that too well to take it personally."

"Not today, I don't," Wallis grumbled, her mind already racing ahead to the next problem. She started walking toward the door to her private office. Turning to Ivy again, she said, "Find Patten for me, will you? I want to make sure he knows he's got all the support he needs."

Ivy buzzed her on the intercom a minute later. "No answer at his house or office, Wallis. He must be on his way."

Wallis glanced at her watch. "Well, keep trying. Maybe we can catch up with him before the session this afternoon." She buzzed off, returning to the newspaper story and trying to shake off the sense of impending doom that had been gathering strength all morning. News was news after all, and Ernie's behavior was just one more political side show. It would all blow over soon enough—she hoped! Still, she had to work at controlling her own sense of doubt as she began to accept some of the phone calls that were flooding the office.

Graham Davis, thoughtful as ever, was one of the first to call. "Ernie's out to get us, I see," he said philosophically. "I knew he was against Patten, but quite frankly, I didn't expect him to launch this kind of attack. The monorail's been in the works for some time. I don't think that's his real problem. I think he's using it to get at Patten—and you."

"I'm sure you're right," Wallis agreed, glad to talk to her friend. "As far as Ernie's concerned, Patten is just another outsider brought in to threaten him. But I'm sure Patten can handle Ernie."

"Well, I hope you're right," Graham said. "We don't want to lose the monorail. It's one of the good things happening these days. In any case, let me know if there's anything I can do. You know I'm behind Patten all the way."

"Thanks, Graham. Thanks a lot." Wallis was grateful for his support. "It means a great deal to me to know I can depend on you. I'll see you this afternoon." Somehow, talking to Graham put the world into perspective again. Wallis calmed down a little and turned her attention to the pile of paperwork on her desk. She dealt with it quickly and efficiently, then made some more calls, rescheduling a meeting with the Delegation for Minority Rights. She had her hands full enough today. Some problems would have to wait. Soon she was caught up in the routine of the office, completely engrossed in her work.

"Mind if I come in?" asked a low voice at the door, and Wallis looked up, surprised to see Sam, his arms filled with bags that obviously contained lunch, judging from the tasty aromas suddenly filling the room.

"Is it that time already?" Wallis asked with disbelief. She had been so busy that she had completely lost track of time.

"On the nose," he assured her as he opened the bags and began putting containers of food on the desk. "I got your favorite—crawfish gumbo from the Cabaret. Have to keep your strength up."

"How did you know my spirits needed bolstering?" Wallis walked around the desk and gave him a hug.

"I read the paper this morning," Sam said matter-of-factly, giving her a kiss. "And whispers of a garbage strike fill the news office."

Wallis brushed her hair out of her face with a distracted gesture. "I haven't even had time to worry about that one." She sat down in one of the big leather chairs.

"Ernie's hot to trot, isn't he? What do you suppose is *really* bothering him?" Sam handed her a bowl of gumbo and a spoon and sat down in the chair across from her.

Wallis looked up at him. Sam was making small talk. That wasn't like him. Something else was on his mind. "Oh, I don't know," she said with a hopeless shrug. "Ernie's so conservative that I expect him to propose street cars any day. Besides, he can't resist the spotlight. You know that." She tasted her lunch. "Mmmm, this is good." She watched Sam stirring his gumbo. "But you didn't come all the way downtown to talk about Ernie. What's up?"

Sam kept on stirring. He hadn't touched it. "You're right, of course. You know me pretty well." He didn't look up.

"Well—what is it?" Wallis had neither the time nor the patience for games, and she sounded irritable.

"I've got some bad news," Sam began. "You're not going to like it."

"It won't be the first bad news I've had today," Wallis said with a chuckle. Sam seemed so miserable that she felt her impatience subside a little. She had no idea what could be troubling him so.

Sam put his bowl of gumbo down on the desk and looked up at Wallis, for the first time meeting her eyes directly. "Graham Davis is a silent partner in the Gulf Coast Development Corporation. He has been for more than twenty years. The president of the company is his nephew." Sam's voice was quiet but he fairly spat out the words, as if he knew there was no way to soften the blow.

Wallis stared at him. She understood the implications. "That's not possible," she said firmly.

"I wish it weren't true," Sam agreed.

"Are you trying to tell me that Graham Davis has been cheating the city for more than twenty years?" Wallis was incredulous.

"That's right," Sam answered, then continued in a

softer tone. "Look, Wally, I know how hard this is for you, but—"

"Don't patronize me. It's not hard for me because I don't believe a word of it. I simply don't believe it. Why, I've known Graham Davis since I was a child. He's my father's best friend and one of my strongest allies. He's the best city councilman we've ever had." She had gotten up from her chair and was walking angrily about the room.

"That may be so," Sam said, a touch of anger creeping into his voice. "But you've got to believe me. I know what I'm talking about. The man's a crook."

Wallis was furious. She didn't want to hear what Sam was telling her. "Don't say that again—not ever!"

"Think about it, Wally. *Why* has he never run for mayor himself? He's popular with the voters. He's got an impeccable record. His civic contributions to this city are exemplary. He's a perfect candidate for mayor. He'd probably win hands down against any opponent. Why does he stay on the city council?" Sam was being persistent.

"That's easy, Sam. He's devoted to his family. It would take more time than he's willing to give." Wallis was sure of that answer.

"I don't think so. I think he knows his financial situation wouldn't withstand the scrutiny of a mayoral campaign. He's never run for mayor because he has too much to hide." Sam was adamant.

"No, that's not true. It can't be true. I don't believe

a word of it." But Sam's argument was a powerful one, and Wallis knew it.

"Come on, Wallis, be reasonable, will you?" Sam pleaded.

Wallis took a deep breath. "Okay, Sam. Reasonable," she relented sarcastically. "Tell me, what kind of proof do you have? Or is that an unreasonable question?"

"No, Wallis, it's not," Sam answered wearily. "Graham's nephew has been having an affair with his secretary. When his wife found out, the secretary was fired. She's my informant. She's only out to hurt the nephew. She didn't even know the information about Graham was important. But when all this business about Patten Roberts and the monorail started making headlines, she began to put two and two together. She still had the keys to the office and came up with some city permits she said Davis had forged. The private eye working with me had the handwriting verified by an expert last night while we were at the movies."

"You knew about this last night?" Wallis could scarcely believe her ears.

"I didn't have any real proof," Sam said, running his hand through his hair. "I kept hoping it wasn't true."

Wallis sat down in the chair to face him. "You should have told me then."

"Would it have made any difference?" Sam asked, his voice flat. He was looking down at the floor.

Wallis sat silent for a minute. She was thinking

about Graham's phone call earlier that morning. The monorail had been important to him. No wonder. Then she sighed, "No, it wouldn't have changed a thing." She took another deep breath. The shock of this news was more than she could deal with in a few short minutes. What she needed was time, time to absorb this, to decide what had to be done.

"Wally," Sam said gently, "I'm sorry." There was genuine regret in his voice.

"It's not your fault, Sam." Wallis was up again, out of her chair. "I need a little time, that's all. I've got to sort this through."

"You've got until the evening paper comes out, the late edition," Sam said, looking past her at the door.

"*Tonight's* paper!" Wallis was stunned. "That's not even twenty-four hours. Surely you can wait until tomorrow to write your story."

Sam shook his head. "The city editor is saving the front page for this story. I can't wait."

"What do you mean, you can't wait?" Wallis all but stamped her foot. "Of course you can. I've got to talk to Graham, at least give him a chance to speak for himself."

"I've already done that, this morning before I came here. He knows what's going on."

"*I* want to talk to him—*before* he's tried in the newspaper. You can give me twenty-four hours, can't you?"

Sam stood up. "It's my job, Wally. It's what I have to do. If I stall this story, there's a good chance some other paper will get it first. This is a woman scorned.

She's telling her story to anyone who will listen. Surely you can understand how important this is to me."

Wallis sat down behind her desk, almost as though she needed to regain the authority of her office. "I only understand one thing, Sam Davenport. If that story comes out in tonight's paper, you and I are finished." Her amber eyes were flashing danger signals.

"That seems clear enough to me," Sam threw back at her. "I thought we were equals, you and I. I thought you understood that my work is as important to me as yours is to you. I see I was wrong. Dead wrong." He started walking to the door. "Now if you'll excuse me, Your Honor, I've got a deadline to meet."

Wallis watched him go, wishing that she could stop this, stop him, but there was nothing she could do. Nothing. She was numb all over. Shock. That's what it was. The pain would come later in great rolling waves. It was going to hurt, all of it—Graham's deceit, his dishonesty, his betrayal. It would hurt. Sam was gone. That would hurt the most. Later. It would hurt later. Now she had work to do. Wallis gathered up her papers and headed for the council chambers. She spoke to no one as she left. She avoided Ivy. She would have to explain later, when she had more facts.

The city council meeting went pretty much as she'd expected, except that Graham Davis was not in his usual seat. If Wallis had had any hope left that Sam was wrong, it died when she saw Graham's empty seat. An innocent man would have faced the charges. Wallis was heartsick, but she managed to preside over the meeting without letting her feelings show. Patten made a brilliant presentation. He promised to answer all questions at the press conference. That kept the meeting short, much to Wallis's relief.

At least the reporters didn't badger her too much when she left the chambers. Ivy had been right. Patten's press conference had bought her some time, but they would be after her soon enough. Wallis headed back to her office, determined to find Graham. She would call him and talk to him. He would tell her what had happened, explain it all to her, help her make some sense of it. But Graham wasn't home. Isabel was surprised to learn that he hadn't been at the council meeting. She had not seen him since noon. Wallis hung up the phone. She didn't know what to do next.

But it turned out not to matter. What would happen next had already begun. Without knocking, Ivy, obviously perturbed, came into her office and closed the door. "Wallis, I hate to be the one to tell you this . . ." she paused, trying to catch her breath.

"What is it?" Wallis was surprised by Ivy's lack of composure. "It can't be that bad."

"Oh, yes, it is," Ivy assured her grimly. "The contract negotiations have broken down. The sanitation workers are officially on strike. Now, Wallis. Right now. And there are reporters outside asking what you're going to do."

Give me strength, Wallis thought. Things can only

get better, she told herself. They certainly couldn't get worse. "Let the reporters in, Ivy," she said briskly. "We can handle this. I know we can. And I think you'd better be prepared to stay late tonight. I'm going to need your help." I *have* to handle this, she thought to herself, suddenly feeling very much alone.

8

Whoa, there," Wallis ordered, tossing her long chestnut hair back over her shoulder as she expertly pulled back on the reins. The high-spirited palomino obeyed reluctantly, his golden mane quivering with anticipation as he pranced in place as if he knew horse and rider made a dazzling sight among the crowd of trail riders and cowboys gathered in front of City Hall for the rodeo parade.

"This all seems a little ridiculous to me, Ivy," Wallis grumbled to her chief aide, who stood beside her. The mayor was always Grand Marshal, and Wallis had agreed months ago to lead the parade that would open the annual Rodeo and Livestock Show. While it had seemed like a good idea at the time, today, with the city in the throes of a crippling garbage strike, it hardly seemed appropriate. She had so many pressing problems that leading a parade was the farthest thing from her mind and, at the moment, it seemed like a dreadful waste of time. It was, however, a long-standing custom and Wallis had been loath to abandon it.

"I know how you feel," Ivy smiled sympathetically. "But it simply has to be done. I know you'd rather be working in the office, but I think this is important —if anything, you need to get out and be around people for a while. And the citizens have a right to expect that of you."

"All right, all right," Wallis agreed, with an air of impatience. Not that she had much choice. Given the garbage strike, which had now been in effect for almost a week, it seemed frivolous for her to be doing something like this, rather than staying at her desk. And always preying at the back of her mind was the disappearance of her good friend Graham Davis.

"Besides," Ivy said, smiling as she looked around at some of the other council members attired alike in Western-cut suits, boots, and Stetson hats and astride horses champing at the bit to get started, "in view of the state of affairs at the moment, it can't hurt any of you to present a unified front."

Wallis looked at her friend, a brief expression of amusement lighting her amber eyes. "You missed your calling, Ivy," she said, laughing. "Think of all the money you could be making in some high-powered public relations firm." She reached down and patted Ivy on the shoulder, to show that she was only joking.

"Public relations?" Ivy sniffed. "Wouldn't touch it with a ten-foot pole. Besides, I do enough public relations work in your office. It hasn't been easy fielding calls about the garbage strike. It makes the Davis business look like a picnic."

Wallis knew she was right. In all the fuss and fury about the sanitation workers' strike, Sam's story about the Gulf Coast Development Corporation and Graham Davis had been upstaged and the subsequent furor relegated to the second and third pages. Wallis had never gotten to talk to Graham. He had simply walked out on everything—his wife, his children, his responsibilities. Wallis's greatest fear, of course, was that he had harmed himself, but as each day passed with no word, she began to worry less and less about that, though routine checks of the city hospitals and morgue continued to be made.

The real story—and everyone knew it—was the strike. It had happened in other major cities, of course, but this was the first time such a strike had occurred here, and Wallis wasn't pleased that it had taken place during her administration. But that was no more than a piece of bad luck, considering the date of the contract renewal. It was bound to happen sooner or later.

A policeman's shrill whistle brought Wallis back to the present, and she realized the parade was forming. It was a cool, clear morning in late February, and Wallis had dressed warmly. She wore a Western-cut beige gabardine trouser suit with a brown silk shirt and a wonderful bow tie made of brown ostrich feathers. She hoped Ivy was right—maybe this would do her good.

When she reached the blocked-off street where the parade was assembling, Wallis was welcomed by the cordial greetings of the other participants. At least they didn't seem to be blaming her personally for the strike, though it couldn't have happened at a worse time—the one weekend when visitors from all over the country would be flocking to the rodeo. She had wanted the city to put on its best face for this annual festivity, and she felt a pang of regret as she looked at the sacks of garbage lining the alleys. This couldn't go on much longer. The strike had to be resolved—and soon!

Word had it that, at any moment, there could be a break in the negotiations. Wallis hoped it would come soon, but she was not optimistic, since she guessed there would be several volleys of compromises before a settlement was reached. She had personally put in a good many hours on the city's first response to the demands made by the sanitation workers, and she thought it a fair offer. Not all the workers' demands had been met—several council members, herself included, felt that the city could not realistically afford some of the benefits—though some had been agreed upon. Wallis knew that there was still a lot of work ahead. There would no doubt be more concessions on both sides, and she knew these deliberations could not be hurried.

Expertly moving alongside Theo Papadakis and

Lamar Steele, Wallis did her best to rise to the occasion. "How'd you get roped into doing this?" she teased, shaking hands with both of them.

As if they were one person, the two of them gestured in Ivy's direction. "I see." Wallis chuckled. "Well, maybe Ivy's wasting her time here—maybe we should have her sitting in on the strike negotiations."

"You mean she's not?" Lamar feigned shock. "No wonder it's taking so long."

Theo moved forward on his horse, obviously having a little trouble keeping him in line. "Surely there's something we can do about that." Both men seemed to understand that this occasion was a painful duty for Wallis, and they appeared to be making a concerted effort at keeping things light-hearted. Wallis turned to give Ivy a glance, but her aide had already disappeared, no doubt heading back to the office. "Ivy *does* get the job done," she said, turning to look at her two companions. "Speaking of getting the job done, that's what the council needs to do. This strike has gone on long enough. I think it's time we settled it, and I'm counting on you two to help."

"You know you've got my help," Lamar said quietly. "I think we simply ought to give the workers what they want—let's face it, in a city this size, we can't afford to be without such a vital city service for so long. And they're long overdue for an increase."

"I couldn't agree with you more," Wallis said warmly. "Though there are some points we need to consider carefully. We'll only be making matters worse if we overspend—that's not doing anyone a favor in the long run." Theo and Lamar were now riding on either side of Wallis, and the horses had finally fallen into step, making it easy for the trio to converse while at the same time they waved and nodded to the crowd beginning to line the streets.

Lamar was not to be so easily defeated. "But some raise in salary is absolutely vital. You'd think that would be obvious to even the most conservative of us."

Surprisingly enough, Theo seemed fairly unconcerned. "Oh, the council members will come around," he said airily, with the confidence of the newly elected. "Just give their constituents time to register their feelings—after this sort of thing goes on for a while, people will be ready to pay anything to have their garbage picked up. I have no doubt that the council will agree to anything reasonable that's presented. It's just a matter of time."

Mulling that over in her mind, Wallis knew Theo was right. Solving most problems was just a matter of time. If only all difficulties could be taken care of so easily. Wallis had one problem that she was sure would never be solved, and that was Sam Davenport.

Damn that man! Just when she thought she had shaken him from her heart and mind, he popped up again, the proverbial bad penny. After their argument last week, Wallis had gone home to find all traces of his presence erased from her house, and the place was sadly empty without him. She had been shocked at the void in her life, not having realized how much she had counted on having him there in the evenings, making popcorn, offering his opinions on the issues of the day, typing late into the night. She'd give anything to hear what Sam had to say about the garbage strike. His insight on political matters was often brilliant, and Wallis missed having him as a sounding board.

But it was more than that—Wallis found that her body seemed to miss him with a memory of its own. Often in the night she would wake reaching for him, only to find that he wasn't there and to remember with painful clarity their bitter parting words. True to his promise, Sam had mailed her the key, and when it had arrived a few days later, Wallis had been stunned at the pain it had caused her. Her father had been right—perhaps her ambitions had cost her too high a price.

The worst part of it all was that Sam hadn't disappeared from her life at all—he was still very much in evidence. At every press conference or public event she had participated in since their final parting, he was there somewhere. It was pure torment. He had even been present at the press conference when she had officially announced the garbage strike.

She remembered that day all too well—she had been calm and composed as usual, but when she looked up and saw his familiar figure slouched against the doorway of the room her heart skipped a beat, and she had to struggle for control. So much had come between them since that lovely beginning on the rooftop. Tears had risen to her eyes, but she covered the moment by asking the assembled reporters not to smoke. Sam stood there through the whole thing watching and listening, and Wallis found it hard not to look for him, not to seek out his blond hair, his blue eyes. When the conference ended, she was grateful that he had left early, not lingering to ask questions about the Gulf Coast Development Corporation and Graham Davis as most of the other reporters had.

But then, he had all the answers, she reminded herself bitterly. He had been in on the scandal from the beginning. He was the first reporter with the news, the first to get a story. That's all that really mattered to him. Not human beings, not decency, not diplomacy—not even *her* feelings. Beating the others to the punch, that's what mattered most to him. A scoop. Unfortunately for her, she had had to learn that the hard way. Twenty-four hours, that's all she had asked. As it turned out, she might as well have asked for the moon. It had been a double betrayal for her—Graham's deceit and Sam's ambition.

She had been so sure that Sam loved her. There *had* been something special there. No one could have faked that. Maybe she was being too hard on him. She knew his job was as important as hers. He didn't have to remind her of that. Maybe they could . . . No, that was absurd. Wallis brought herself up short. Their professions were not compatible. It wouldn't work, not over the long haul. But she missed him, and there seemed to be no way in the world to get him back.

"Hey, Wallis," Theo said softly at her side. "What's the matter? Your heart's not in this."

Wallis snapped out of her reverie and noticed that both Theo and Lamar were showing real concern about her long silence. She looked around, realizing her mind had been a million miles away.

"Oh," she said, dismissing their concern with a smile and a cheery wave to the crowd, "it's depressing, seeing all the garbage."

Lamar looked around at the streets and sidewalks. "I don't see any, Wallis. How can you see any garbage with all these people?" He peered at the sidewalks earnestly.

"No, no," Wallis reassured him. "I'm just thinking of what will be left after this parade is over." She knew she sounded like a pessimist, but she couldn't help it.

"Oh, come on, Wallis." Even Theo seemed caught up in the holiday spirit of the rodeo parade. "I told you, it's only a matter of time."

"I know it is." Wallis grinned, a forced effort. "Maybe tomorrow this will all be over." In her heart, she fervently hoped so, but she knew that the real cause of her pain was something that wouldn't go away—not for a long, long time. Maybe not ever.

Determined not to be caught daydreaming again, Wallis turned her full attention to the parade and the rodeo festivities. It wasn't long before the group reached the Astrodome, and they rode through the gates to the actual site of the rodeo.

The opening ceremony was colorful as the trail riders circled the huge indoor arena. Many had come from as far as Santa Fe and Colorado and Arizona, on horseback and in covered wagons of all shapes and sizes. Wallis led the way on her magnificent horse, flanked on either side by flag bearers carrying the red, white, and blue American and Texas flags. Wallis was no novice equestrian. As a child she had spent weekends and vacations on the sprawling acres of the ranch her father owned in the Texas Hill Country, and when she was a kid she'd been more at home on a horse than in her own living room. Even now, when Wallis wanted to get away from it all, the Lazy S ranch provided an idyllic haven from the city. The horses stabled there were always ready to be ridden, and Wallis found nothing more relaxing than a long ride across the rolling Texas hills.

As it turned out, this particular ride was not so relaxing. The rodeo fans were not all enthusiastic supporters of Wallis, and it was soon obvious that the rodeo was being used that evening as a political forum for those who were angry at the current administration for its handling of the garbage strike. A few boos and catcalls were hurled at Wallis, Theo, and Lamar as they rode by row after row of spectators. There were even a few banners that reflected the angry mood of many of the city's residents. The garbage strike was foremost in everyone's mind.

Wallis had expected as much—the crowd reflected her own mood. By the time she had completed her duties as Grand Marshal, she was glad that the ordeal was behind her. For an awful moment, as she left the arena, she wondered if she had taken on more than she could handle. Maybe I can't do this job, she thought. I can't manage my personal affairs, what makes me think I can run one of the biggest cities in the country? A small voice inside her spoke with authority, reminding her of her goals. Of course you can, it said, this is what you were meant to do, what you've always wanted. Your personal life will take care of itself. You take care of the city. With an aching loneliness, Wallis realized that that was indeed all she had to care about at the moment.

Handing over the reins of her horse to one of the rodeo clowns, she said to Theo in a low voice, "We should have known that was coming. I can't blame them, but I wish there were some way for them to understand that we hate this strike as much as anyone."

Lamar took her arm and led her in the direction of the elevators to the Director's Club where they were to have lunch with the rodeo dignitaries. "It's not your fault, Wallis. You've got to remember that. And you're doing everything in your power to resolve this mess. You know as well as I do that unless a person has been directly involved in negotiations like these, it's impossible to understand how complicated it all is."

"I know—" Wallis began, trying not to sound as defeated as she felt. She had stopped walking and was no longer following Lamar.

"Besides, not everyone out there was against

you." Theo came up behind them. His horse had proved troublesome throughout the morning and he had trailed Wallis and Lamar. "You've obviously got a lot of supporters, Wallis. You mustn't let a handful of dissenters get you down."

"Oh, I know, and I thank you both, really I do." She smiled warmly at the two men who were beside her. "And I'm not going to let it get me down. But what I *am* going to do is make my appearance with the directors and skip out as soon as possible. I want you two to cover for me. I've got entirely too much work I want to do to waste any more of the day." She spoke with such determination that there was little her colleagues could do except agree to her plan and promise to help her get away when the time was right. They took the private elevator up to the large suite of sky boxes that served as the Director's Club during the rodeo. As they got off the elevator, Wallis saw a group of reporters and felt her heart skip a beat as she automatically scanned the sea of faces for Sam. Her heart caught in her throat as she thought she spotted his rangy form in the crowd. But it wasn't him.

Strangely, she felt disappointed. Looking at him, even under these awful circumstances, would be better than not seeing him at all. Or so she thought. At that moment, she would have given anything for a masculine shoulder to lean on, a man to go home to that night.

As the threesome made their way through the crowd, Wallis talked with those people she knew, though she refused to comment on the garbage strike. This was neither the time nor the place, she told herself wisely.

Thirty minutes or so later, Wallis decided she had had enough of the rodeo festivities and felt that she had done all that could be expected of her. She looked around for Lamar, thinking she'd say good-bye to him, but when she spotted him, she saw that he was near the buffet table with his vivacious wife, Jessica, who coached the city's professional basket-ball team. Wallis felt a pang of jealousy as she looked at the happy couple, and as much as Wallis would have loved to speak to Jessica, she was determined not to stay at this party any longer than was neces-sary. With a farewell wave to Lamar, who winked at her in return, Wallis slipped unnoticed out through one of the back doors.

Once outside in the corridor, Wallis heaved a sigh of relief. As much as she enjoyed her office and the responsibilities of being mayor, she was glad, for the moment, to be out of the public eye. Luckily, she found the service elevator empty. Alone at last, she thought to herself as the doors closed. For once, she didn't feel like being stared at and she put on a white silk scarf and a pair of dark glasses. It wasn't much of a disguise, but she knew from experience that it would help.

As she made her way through the crowd and out of the Astrodome, Wallis felt her spirits lift slightly. She had been doing what had been expected of her all day, and for the moment she felt like a child playing hooky from school. It was a beautiful afternoon, and the parking lots surrounding the stadium were filled with cars and chartered buses. A group of school children in uniform walked past her, the boisterous chants of the youngsters a delightful change from the serious tone of politics that had followed her all that day. She waved at them and watched as they gathered noisily around a balloon man, some finding change in their pockets to buy his wares.

Wallis smiled to herself and began walking down the concrete ramp to a row of taxis she saw parked along the curb. Over to her right, she saw that, as usual, a carnival was set up outside the entrance to the livestock show. The noisy rides decorated with brightly colored flags bobbled up and down, and Wallis stopped to watch. The double Ferris wheel lurched forward and stopped to let on new passengers, and a couple in the top seat waved to a group of children below. The temptation was too great.

Maybe I will, she whispered to herself. As she hurried toward the carnival, she knew all her problems would be waiting for her when she got back but she also knew that ten minutes wouldn't hurt one way or the other. It had been years since she had ridden a Ferris wheel. Somehow, this was one ride she couldn't pass up. She would take this moment for herself.

Wallis joined the short line. While she waited, she took a dollar bill from her purse and tucked it into her pants pocket, returning the strap of her bag to her shoulder. She noted with satisfaction that no one had recognized her, and for a few minutes she felt like a different person. The next moment she was caught completely off guard. Just as she was handing over her money to buy a ticket, a deep voice spoke over her shoulder to the man selling tickets.

"Make that two, will you?"

Wallis was astonished, as she turned to identify the source of the voice, to find Sam looking down at her, his hand on her shoulder. She didn't have time to argue. The vendor did as he was told, giving the two tickets to Sam, who had stepped forward and neatly intercepted them.

"I beg your pardon," Wallis said haughtily, amazed that her voice was working at all.

Sam had on jeans and a plaid shirt and a Western-cut camel-colored jacket. He was most handsome, she thought, when he was casually dressed.

"That is, if you don't mind," he said with a grin, belatedly giving her a chance to refuse.

"Oh, not at all," Wallis said, not without some sarcasm. She obviously had no choice. The familiar touch of his hand on her arm brought quick tears to her eyes; she was not prepared for her strong reaction. "Though you might have waited your turn like everyone else." She hoped her voice sounded casual.

Sam didn't appear to be listening. He pushed open the low metal gate in front of them and guided her through to an empty seat, swinging slightly from the last ride. He sat down first and, holding out his hand, helped her aboard. When she sat down, he put his arm around her shoulders as the operator locked the heavy metal bar in place.

"I feel as if I just paid for my own kidnapping," Wallis said with mock indignation. She couldn't help responding to Sam's maneuver with good spirits. There was always something about him that she found irresistible. It was hard to remain aloof.

"Think what a mighty ransom I could hold you for," he said, merriment in his eyes as he leaned over to kiss her. At that moment, the last passenger having been made secure, the wheel began to turn slowly, the seats swaying back and forth.

"I don't know about that," Wallis quipped gloomily. "I'm not winning any popularity contests right now. It might be that no one would pay it—or haven't you been keeping up with city politics?"

"You know better than that," Sam returned. Removing her dark glasses and putting them in his pocket, he pulled her even closer, his eyes searching hers, looking for something beyond their conversation.

"Yes, I guess I do," Wallis whispered urgently, her mouth moving up to meet his. This kiss was more intense than the first, and the gentle sway of the Ferris wheel matched the leap her heart made.

"I've missed you," she began, not knowing where else to start but with the obvious. She took off the silk scarf and let her long hair fall loose.

"And I've missed you," Sam answered. He kissed her again, gently. They were at the top of the circle and were beginning the descent. "It's not easy getting you alone."

Wallis laughed, thinking of their first meeting. "You've got a pretty good knack for it, I'd say. Where did you come from anyway? Have you been following me?" Something about the ride put them beyond ordinary space and time, and they were able to talk, for the moment at least, as though they had never quarreled.

"Of course not," Sam said, indignant at the question. "I've spent most of the day covering the livestock show, and I was coming out when I saw you walk over to the Ferris wheel. That's not much of a disguise, you know." He picked up the white scarf, letting its silky folds fall through his fingers.

"I wasn't trying to hide from you," Wallis said earnestly. The Ferris wheel was taking them up again, and Wallis felt butterflies in her stomach.

Sam put the white scarf over his hand and held it up like a flag. "What do you say we call a truce?" His voice was soft. He didn't look at her.

"There's nothing I'd like better." Wallis knew that was true. She reached over and put her hand on his. The Ferris wheel went round and round, and for the next several minutes, Wallis and Sam were in a world all their own. Nothing mattered except the gentle touch of their lips pressing together or the sound of their hearts racing as they were carried high above the rodeo grounds.

The ride was nearly over, and the Ferris wheel began making its stops, letting the passengers go, two by two. Realizing they had only a few minutes left, Wallis and Sam both began talking at once.

"Oh, Sam—"

"You know—" he began.

Laughing at their joint impatience, each stopped, waiting for the other to begin again. But Wallis was most determined to speak her mind. She wanted Sam to know that nothing else mattered except that they be together.

"I was wrong, Sam. Your job is as important as mine. I was too quick to lose my temper. Just because you were headstrong was no reason for me to react as I did." She was relieved to have that out in the open.

But the look on Sam's face was one of dismay. "Headstrong? Wally, don't you understand? I did what I had to do—*when* I had to do it. Surely you must know that by now."

"It doesn't matter, Sam. None of it matters."

"Oh, but it does matter," Sam said, a coolness in his voice. "It matters very much. I need you to respect my work as I respect yours."

"But how *can* I respect work that has so little compassion for human lives?" Wallis wished she could make him understand.

"You think because I wanted to print the truth that I have no compassion?" Sam was as persuasive as he was angry. "What about the voters, Wally? It seems to me that you've been putting one person and his family above the people you've been elected to serve."

"Sam, that's not fair," Wallis cried, knowing there was some truth in Sam's accusation. The Ferris wheel lurched forward again, this time bringing them to the ground. There was nothing she could do in that instant to change his mind.

The Ferris wheel operator reached across them and unlocked the bar that held them in place. "You folks enjoy the ride?" The question was perfunctory; he was busy doing his job and he didn't really expect an answer.

Sam stood up and gave Wallis his hand to help her out. The spell had been broken, and these last movements were formal and obligatory.

"Sam, I'm sorry," Wallis began. "I wish—"

"I'm sorry too, Wally. More than you'll ever know."

There was nothing else to say. It had all been said. They walked to the gate and Sam turned to go. "Thanks for the ride, Wally." He touched her face with his hand and wiped away a single tear that fell on her cheek. "I'm sorry it had to end."

There was a moment when Wallis could have reached out and stopped him, when she could have said something that would have made a difference, but the words wouldn't come. Silence was her answer, her foe, her downfall. It was that simple. It was that complicated. And so she watched as he pushed open the low metal gate and headed back to the livestock show. Her heart caught in her throat, choked with the words that would not be said. As she turned toward the row of waiting taxis, she knew that never, as long as she lived, would she love anyone the way she loved Sam Davenport. She put on her dark glasses, hoping to hide the tears.

9

Wallis looked out of her window at the reflecting pond in front of City Hall, a sight that usually gave her pleasure. But today there was no joy in it for her. A crowd was milling about the edges of the pond, and the faces of the people were unhappy. It was a cold gray morning, and the gathering clouds indicated that another drizzly day was in the offing. The threatening weather seemed to reinforce the displeasure of the throng. Though one or two individuals seemed to be in charge, the rest of the group walked around aimlessly, their faces a study in discontent. Even the normally calm waters of the pond seemed dark and foreboding.

She watched the scene with interest and resignation. The sleek black and white pinstripe suit she wore was hand tailored, and the white silk shirt was clasped at the throat with a handsome cameo that had been her grandmother's. Her long chestnut hair was tied back with a narrow black ribbon. Her extraordinary beauty was not dampened by the burdens of the moment, though her heart was heavy.

Despite her efforts to remain detached, her sympathy went out to the people assembled in the cold grayness outside. It had been inevitable that this would happen. She wished she had good news for them, but right now she didn't have any news at all.

Wallis heard the door open and knew that Ivy had entered the office. "I'm sorry, Wallis," she heard her friend say. "But I'm afraid we're going to have to go out there and talk to them sooner or later." Wallis was grateful for the sound of that "we" and knew that Ivy meant it—any problem that involved Wallis and the mayor's office was a shared one. She straightened her shoulders and turned to give her friend a tired smile.

"I know," Wallis said. "I just keep hoping that something will happen—that the negotiations today will be the final ones." She struggled to keep her voice level but finally gave in, deciding to let some of her anger out. "It's all so senseless—I've worked and worked to bring this strike to an end, and nothing I've done has been enough. It's so frustrating." She turned to look out of the window again. "And now this—of course the citizens are angry. I don't blame them. I'm angry too. I hope that some of the council holdouts are watching this. Let them see the trouble they've caused."

Ivy came to her side and joined her vigil at the window. "They *have* come around finally, though, and you don't know for sure that the latest offer hasn't been accepted. The negotiations are still underway. If you like, I could call over to the sanitation department and see how things are going. The meeting should be almost over." She made a move toward the phone, anxious to do anything that might ease the mayor's mind.

"No, no." Wallis smiled gently. "I know they'll call as soon as they're finished. It's just that it's taking so long. The workers know that this is our final and best offer, and I think they'll accept it. Playing the waiting game is something I've never been very good at."

At that, Ivy had to smile. "You're telling me? I'm the one who held your hand while we were waiting for the election results, remember?" She laughed quietly.

Wallis joined in, grateful for Ivy's humor. But a glance out the window reminded her of the tenseness of the situation, and her glum mood returned. "That seems so long ago, Ivy. It really does."

During the last few days, Wallis had done everything in her power to bring the strike to a close—and had paid the price in lack of sleep. She had met virtually nonstop with advisors, sanitation department representatives, city council members, and negotiators—all of whom were trying to resolve the issues according to their own ideas. It hadn't been easy, for each side had certain points in its favor.

The sanitation workers were long overdue for a raise and everyone knew it, Wallis included. Up until the strike, it had been one of the most smoothly run city departments, and for that reason no one had expected such long, difficult negotiations—it had been taken for granted that a modest salary increase would satisfy the workers. But pent-up anger had taken its toll, and the workers were asking for a much higher increase, though Wallis thought that it was justified. Now they were virtually holding the city hostage until their demands were met.

On the other hand, some council members were reluctant to alter the city budget to allow for the pay increase, even though they knew the adjustment was necessary. The budget had allowed for the usual cost-of-living increase but for little beyond that. The council had been evenly split on the issue, though the older, more conservative members were the most recalcitrant, saying they weren't about to give in to such outrageous demands. Wallis suspected them of secretly enjoying the drama and the attention. But the city could take only so much of this, and she had known that it was just a matter of time until the force of public opinion brought them around, as it finally had. Wallis took little comfort in the fact that the fault was not with her administration and that everyone knew which council members were opposed to the rate increase.

The pain of losing her good friend and confidante Graham Davis had not diminished. No one had heard a word from him, not even his wife Isabel who was, from all reports, sick with worry. The shame must be too great, Wallis thought sadly as she thought of his otherwise impeccable career now ruined by corruption. Why had he done it, she wondered. Why? He had done so many good things for the city. What kind of pressures had it taken to bend so strong a man? Wallis shook her head. Maybe he wasn't a good man, she reminded herself sternly. Maybe he was a fraud through and through. Maybe she had never really known him at all. Maybe she had only thought she had. She had dealt with the situation as best she could and was pleased that she had been able to act coolly and impartially. She had appointed someone to take Graham's place during the interim period and had made sure that a special election would be set up as quickly as possible.

The problem facing her now was different but equally complex. She had spent all day in meetings concerning the strike and now, for the first time, she actually felt hopeful. She had done her best to work out a compromise, had tried to set up generous fringe benefits to compensate for a moderate salary increase. Even the most stubborn council members had seen the wisdom of her plan and, finally buckling to public pressure, had passed it. It was to be presented to representatives of the sanitation department that afternoon, and Wallis was spending some nervous hours awaiting the results.

Oh, the timing is all wrong—it's all off, Wallis thought. Just when she'd hoped that she would have good news for everyone, the people had put together this protest. Not that she blamed them. She was tired of looking at her overflowing garbage cans too and wondering when someone would be along to empty them. She had hoped that the problem would be resolved in time to defuse the public's anger, but it looked as if she would be bearing the brunt of it. It wasn't that she didn't want to go down and speak to the crowd, but she wished she had something to tell them. Tears of frustration filled her eyes, and she smashed her fist against the desk in anger. She stared at the phone, willing it to ring.

Ivy followed her gaze, not wanting to break the silence that enveloped the office. Wallis gave her a look, aware that Ivy knew exactly what she was thinking. "Only a little longer, Wallis," Ivy said reassuringly. "The meeting's been going on for over an hour. It's bound to be over soon—it has to be."

Wallis sat down at her desk and began reading the letters Ivy had prepared for her signature, her face set in a determined expression. "I'll be all right, Ivy," she said quietly, her tone all business. "I'll finish these up. Let me know when the group outside asks to see me."

Ivy had turned to leave when there was a knock at the door. Before Wallis or Ivy could answer the knock, the door opened and they saw Patten Roberts' grinning face.

"I realize your minds aren't really on transit problems at the moment," he said, seeing that they were both in a black mood, "but I thought I could provide some comic relief." He looked around expectantly.

"Sure thing," Ivy said briskly. "I'll get some coffee and be right back."

Wallis was glad to see the young head of the Metropolitan Transit System. She'd had little contact with him lately, since the garbage strike had taken up most of her time. She had heard favorable reports about his progress, though, and knew that he was doing a good job in spite of the scandal brewing over the Gulf Coast Development Corporation and the monorail contract. "What's up, Patten?" she asked, grateful for the distraction.

"I've got some good news and some bad news," Patten said jovially. "Ready?"

The words "bad news" weren't what Wallis wanted to hear at the moment. "Okay," she said, steeling herself. "Let's hear it."

Patten made himself comfortable in one of the wingback chairs as Ivy entered with three cups of coffee and took a seat opposite him. "The good news is that some of our new buses are beginning to arrive, so service should be improving quickly." He paused a moment for effect. "The bad news is that the bus drivers won't use the buses to pick up the garbage. I've asked them and asked them, but they're not interested in working overtime."

This idea was so unexpected that Wallis and Ivy looked at each other and began to giggle. As Patten looked on in undisguised astonishment, the giggles turned to outright laughter. This was more than he had bargained for. They laughed until tears ran down their cheeks, and as Wallis struggled to regain her composure, she realized how tense she had been all afternoon. It was good to laugh. She hadn't laughed so hard in a long time, not since Sam . . . But she wasn't going to think about that now.

"It was only a little joke," Patten said apologetically. "I didn't expect to bring the house down." He stared at the two women, both wiping tears from their eyes.

Wallis looked at him and started laughing all over again. "I know," she said when she had calmed down, "but there hasn't been much joking around here lately, as I'm sure you can imagine. We needed a good laugh. Thank you for providing it."

Ivy had composed herself as well. "Wallis is right," she said with a grin. "We haven't had anything to joke about in a long time."

"Well, I do have some other news," Patten began, finally getting to the point. "We have the new buses—and they are improving service. That should ease us over the rough spots until the contraflow lanes are set up and while the monorail's under construction. I'm looking for other companies to take over the Gulf Coast Development Corporation's contract. They aren't the only contractors in town, you know. Now that we have a little more time, the architects and planners have come up with some great new additions to the plans. As a matter of fact, we'll be going over them at the board meeting sometime next week, and then if all goes well, I'll present them to the city council shortly thereafter. How does that sound?"

Wallis had known that Patten was good and that he was a fast worker, but she hadn't expected this—it was exactly the kind of news she needed to hear at that moment when nothing else seemed to be working. "Sounds great," she said enthusiastically, experiencing once again the excitement she always felt when a problem was nearing solution. "Let's see what you've got."

Patten unrolled the large sheaf of papers he'd been carrying when he entered the office and crossed to Wallis's desk, Ivy following close behind. For a long time, the three of them pored over the suggested plans, questioning, praising, and criticizing. This was the kind of situation that brought out the best in Wallis. Developing a workable transit system for the city had long been a dream of hers, and she felt fortunate to have found someone as bright and as dedicated as Patten. He had put a lot of energy into his plans and they seemed sound in every detail, from the proposed route of the monorail to the new improved schedule of city bus services.

Wallis had momentarily pushed the strike out of her mind and was genuinely enjoying the challenge of the work when one of her secretaries knocked on the door. The attractive redhead looked in a bit timidly. "The people outside are asking for you, Ms. Mayor," she said softly. "They don't seem upset or anything, but they've sent a representative in to ask if you would come out and speak with them. It's starting to rain, and some of the people are getting restless and want to go home."

Wallis, Ivy, and Patten all looked out of the window and saw the steady gray drizzle outside. "Right, Phyl," Wallis said briskly. "Tell them I'll be right out. There haven't been any calls from the sanitation department, I take it?"

"I'm sorry," Phyl answered. "Not yet. Ivy said I was to let you know immediately if there were, but we haven't heard a word yet. I'll tell that representative you'll be right out." She quickly withdrew.

Wallis looked at Patten and Ivy and squared her shoulders. "Time to face the music," she said resolutely, reaching for the black coat that hung over the back of her chair. She shrugged into it easily, thinking that she would soon be grateful for its warmth in the drizzle outside. She wasn't looking forward to this. "Here are your letters, Ivy," she said matter-of-factly, pushing a sheaf of papers across the desk. "Patten, I like your ideas and I'll look forward to discussing them in greater detail. Set up an appointment with Ivy for tomorrow, all right? I'm on my way."

"I'll come too," Ivy insisted, but Wallis held up a hand in protest.

"No, you stay here to answer the phone. Let me know as soon as something happens. I can handle this. Just keep your fingers crossed. We're right down to the wire on this one. But we'll make it, Ivy. If only I had some good news for that crowd . . ."

"You will soon," Ivy said solemnly, as if making a promise. "I know it." She and Patten followed Wallis out of the office, and Ivy took up her post at the phone on her desk. Wallis turned to shake hands with Patten and saw the determined look on his face.

"I'm coming with you," he said firmly.

"I'm not sure that's wise," Wallis began, but he stopped her.

"It may not be wise," Patten quipped, "but it's certainly convenient—it's on the way to my office. What's a few more minutes out in the rain?" He grinned broadly, and Wallis sensed there would be no talking him out of it.

"All right," she said quietly, "and thanks."

As they entered the hallway, Wallis spotted a group of reporters standing near the bank of elevators. She threw her shoulders back and walked toward them with a determined step. Might as well get it over with, she thought, grateful for Patten's presence. As the reporters caught sight of her, they rushed forward, besieging her with questions about the strike, but Wallis steadfastly refused to comment, saying that she would answer all their questions after she'd met with the group outside.

Thankfully, an elevator arrived, and the reporters crowded in with Wallis and Patten for the short ride down. They sensed they weren't going to get a word out of the mayor and instead began to plague Patten with questions about the work his office was doing. Wallis admired the skillful way he handled the questions. She took the few moments' respite to collect her thoughts, trying to decide what she would say to the crowd. She was grateful for one thing at least. Sam was not among this group of reporters. That would have been the last straw. And that's one problem you can't solve, she reminded herself firmly, trying to concentrate on what was ahead of her.

* * *

Wallis took a deep breath as the elevator stopped at the first floor. Here we go, she thought in anticipation. Patten squeezed her arm as they stepped out of the elevator, and Wallis flashed him a smile. They headed for the front doors of City Hall, Wallis bracing herself for what could only be considered an unpleasant task.

"Wallis! Wallis! Your Honor!" called a voice behind her, and Wallis turned to see a breathless Ivy, who was nevertheless smiling broadly. "Could I have a word with you?"

"Excuse me, folks," Wallis said to the reporters, who were eyeing the two women curiously. "I'll be right with you."

"What is it, Ivy?" she asked when the two women were out of earshot. "Good news?"

"The best!" Ivy rushed on. "The sanitation workers have accepted the offer, the contracts have been signed, and the emergency crews are leaving to go to work. They'll have this mess cleared up before you know it."

"Thank God!" Wallis breathed a heartfelt sigh of relief. This had been a close one. "Thanks, Ivy. Now I *know* I can handle this." Patten had walked over but was hanging back hesitantly, as if he couldn't wait to hear but was reluctant to intrude. "Come on, Patten," Wallis said, sensing that he felt left out. "Let's go tell them the good news!" Smiling, the three of them walked past the reporters through the front door of City Hall, where a microphone had been set up under the portico to give Wallis some volume and shelter from the rain.

Gazing down at the crowd at the bottom of the steps, Wallis saw Sam immediately. He was standing at the edge of the crowd dressed in a tan all-weather coat, and her thoughts flew immediately to Humphrey Bogart in Casablanca. Quickly she centered her thoughts on the job at hand. This was no time to let her heart take control.

Taking the microphone off its stand, she walked down into the crowd to announce the good news. As she had expected, the crowd let out a cheer and, after a short round of pertinent questions, they began to disperse. Wallis understood they were glad to hear the good news and were ready to get out of the bad weather and go back home. That's exactly what she intended to do, the minute she had all the loose ends tied up. Now maybe her life could get back to normal and she could get some sleep. All in a day's work, she thought, as she turned to go back into City Hall. But she had forgotten her promise to the reporters, and they were waiting there on the steps, microphones and notepads in hand.

This time Sam was part of the group, and Wallis had to use every ounce of self-control she could muster to keep from looking at him. She could feel his eyes on her, and she was determined not to let herself be sidetracked, not even for a moment. This was important and it was no time for her private life to intrude. Besides, he was only doing his job. There was nothing personal about his being there.

Wallis answered all the reporters' questions with

poise and confidence, for once grateful that all three television stations were represented, as that insured that the news would go out that evening. It was a pleasant press conference, without the usual tension that Wallis felt at being paraded before the public eye, but still she was glad when it came to a close. She had not forgotten for one moment that Sam was there. Finally the last question was answered, and all the reporters were obviously eager to get off and make deadlines—all but one.

Sam simply stood there, his face inscrutable. He waited until they were alone before he spoke. "Congratulations," he said softly. "I'm very happy this all turned out so well for you."

"Thanks, Sam," she returned, more formally than she had intended. "I think it turned out well for everyone." She made an effort to keep her voice under control, but what she wanted to do was reach out for him, apologize—anything to bring him back into her life again. But she couldn't. At that moment, the clouds opened and it began to rain in earnest. Wallis rushed for the doorway, half expecting him to follow her. But when she turned around to look for him, he was gone, walking slowly through the pouring rain away from City Hall.

"Here's looking at you, kid," she thought to herself in silent tribute. The moment was gone. She could have saved it, but she hadn't said or done the right thing. Even now she felt she should be chasing him. But she couldn't—she just couldn't. She leaned against the doorway, the adrenalin that had kept her going the previous half-hour draining away, leaving her tired and spent. She blinked back a tear. So that's that, she thought. But she stood there for a long time, gazing after the solitary figure walking away in the rain.

10

The crowd cheered as Wallis drew back her arm and threw out the first baseball of the season. The ball arched high in the air, seemed to hesitate a fraction of a second, then dropped to the hands of the catcher. Wallis was delighted to see her pitch reach its target. All those summers playing softball hadn't been for nothing. She hadn't lost her touch!

"Whooee!" Hank Hayes let out a long whistle. The portly owner of the Mavericks was impressed with the accuracy of her pitch. He stood up beside Wallis, joining the crowd in its appreciative applause. "You may be in the wrong profession, Ms. Mayor. Ever think about joining the big time?"

Wallis laughed. She was having fun. "I've played a little baseball in my time, don't think I haven't," she said as she waved to the Astrodome crowd. She couldn't help remembering the last time she had been in this stadium. The hostile protestors that opening day of the rodeo bore no resemblance to this friendly gathering. It had been more than a month since the garbage strike was settled, and Wallis's popularity had never been greater. This day was all hers.

"Wallis used to pitch a mean game," her father said proudly. Judge and Mrs. Carmichael were sitting in the row behind Wallis and the Hayeses, and her dad had leaned forward to contribute to the conversation.

"Don't think I've forgotten that for one minute," Hank said, beaming. "Remember who gave her her first bat and ball?" Turning to Wallis, he continued, "You wouldn't consider coming out for practice one of these days, would you?"

Wallis sat down in the red plush seat and laughed. "You'd better be careful about what you say. I might take you up on that." She flashed a grateful smile at her father, but her attention was claimed by the elegant woman at her right.

Mrs. Hayes reached over and gave Wallis an affectionate pat. "They could do worse, you know. You might be just what this team needs to win a few ball games for a change." The white-haired wife of the team's owner spoke to Wallis in a conspiratorial tone that was obviously meant to be overheard.

"Now, Mama," Hank said plaintively, "we're going to have a good year, you wait and see. Bubba Johnson's been breaking all sorts of records . . ."

"I know, I know," she retorted sarcastically, "and Riley Brooks's retirement won't hurt a bit either."

Wallis settled back in her seat, thoroughly enjoying the friendly banter of two of the city's most colorful characters. This was one honorary occasion she had been looking forward to. Ruth and Henry Hayes were long-time friends of the Carmichaels, and Wallis had grown up listening to Ruthie play straight man to Hank's relentless optimism. The couple's disagreements concerning the management of the baseball team were famous, but Wallis knew it was all part of the show.

It was a Friday afternoon in April, the day of the first game of the season. Wallis had chosen the occasion to break out her spring wardrobe. The white linen suit was cut in the straight, classic lines she liked so much, and the cream-colored silk shirt was fastened at the throat with a bow tie of apricot silk that brought out the rich tones of her chestnut hair. She was every inch a lady—which may have accounted for the little ripple of surprise that marked the crowd's response when she threw out the first ball with such skill.

Things were going well for Wallis. The dark days that had opened her term were behind her now, and while she knew better than to expect all clear sailing from here on out, she was enjoying some respite from the political turmoil that had plagued her first months in office. The garbage strike was no more than a bad memory, and the skill and diplomacy with which she had managed the disastrous affair had given her reputation a solid boost. Patten Roberts had presented a basic plan for the new bus system, and his brilliant and eloquent defense of the monorail system—coupled with hard facts—had been persuasive. The press was giving him good reviews, and it looked as though the council would give him the go-ahead, Ernie Dayton notwithstanding. The special commission investigating the Gulf Coast Development Corporation was expected to make a full report to the council sometime in the next several weeks, though it didn't appear likely that anything new would be revealed. The legal proceedings could, of course, take years. Graham seemed to have disappeared for good, and it was generally assumed that he had vanished rather than face up to a possible jail sentence.

Wallis had every reason to be pleased with her life. Everything seemed to be going her way, as one by one the goals she had set for herself were achieved. Certainly, she still had her hands full—the police department was launching a new public relations campaign, and at her suggestion a civilian board was studying the possibility of a change in the military design of the uniform. There was to be a ballot for a new bond issue soon for the formation of several hundred acres of new parkland in the city . . . the list went on and on.

No one looking at the beautiful, poised, and self-sufficient woman would have guessed at the sadness in her heart, a sadness she kept well hidden. The truth was that Wallis lived in a state of constant, aching loneliness for Sam. She had tried to push him out of her heart and out of her mind, but she only missed him more each day. She hadn't seen him since that fateful day in the rain when she had announced the settlement of the strike. There had been several stories with his by-line in the weeks that followed, but he was no longer part of the group of reporters that covered City Hall. She assumed he had another assignment; probably he had requested it, and she couldn't blame him. But she couldn't keep from searching crowds for his blond hair, his blue eyes.

If she had hoped time would heal the pain, she was sadly disappointed. Her triumphs were empty victories, her success, small consolation. She was far too professional, however, to let this show, and only Ivy had an inkling of the disappointment Wallis felt so keenly. Instead, Wallis redoubled her efforts and worked tirelessly and cheerfully, determined to fill the void at the center of her life. This afternoon was no exception. Wallis watched the game with avid concentration, enjoying the company of her friends.

Before she knew it, it was the bottom of the eighth inning, and the Mavericks were ahead by only two runs. It had been an exciting game, nip and tuck all the way. The bases were loaded. Joe Phillips, the Mavericks' hard-hitting first baseman, hit the ball out of the field.

"Would you look at that, Judge!" Hank shouted.

"A home run!" was the excited answer. The crowd came alive. The Mavericks were clearly in charge now and proved it by allowing the visitors only one run in the top of the ninth.

"I can't tell you how much I've enjoyed this," Wallis said with genuine pleasure as they prepared to go to the Hayeses' skybox for a postgame party. She realized that what she was saying was completely true. "I'd forgotten how much fun it is to go to a baseball game. It's been years since I've been to one."

"Well, we'll just have to see what we can do about that, my dear. You work entirely too hard. All work and no play, you know." Mrs. Hayes shook her head sternly. "That just won't do."

Wallis couldn't have agreed with her more. Even so, the day was not all play. As usual, she was "on stage" even at the party. But the excitement of the game had seduced her, and she was enjoying herself. The party was a lively one; everyone was glad to start the season with such a solid victory. Lamar Steele was there with Jessica, and they exchanged a few pleasantries. Wallis enjoyed her friendship with them but found it difficult not to be envious of their happiness. It was another poignant reminder of Sam and the good times they had shared. She was relieved when their conversation was interrupted, and she found herself gradually moving around the room, talking with old friends, making new ones.

She was deep in conversation with a friend she hadn't seen since high school when her dad came up with the afternoon paper in his hand. "Have you seen this, Wallis?" He was holding the paper open to a second-page story about Graham Davis. "Finally, someone's gotten around to remembering some of the good things Graham did for this city." He handed the paper to Wallis and turned to greet her companion. "Hello, Daphne. How are those three kids?"

While Daphne filled him in, Wallis skimmed the lead story on the editorial page. She guessed it would have to do with her appointment of someone to serve in Graham's seat until there could be an election. Her interest quickened when she saw that the reporter was Sam Davenport.

The headline was, "Politics Takes Heavy Toll," Wallis noted as she skimmed the story. Sam had never been more eloquent as he wrote of the pressures that impinged daily on the lives of public servants and cited the long list of civic contributions Graham had made to the life of the city. The story did not negate the wrong Graham had done but reminded readers that it was not a simple matter. Now that it was time to replace him, it was important that Davis be remembered for the good as well as the bad.

Reading it brought back all of Wallis's mixed feelings about Sam, the Gulf Coast Development Corporation, and Graham's role in the fiasco. It was a well-written, compassionate article, and she could scarcely believe Sam was the author, remembering the single-mindedness with which he had brought Graham's involvement with the corporation out into the open. She thought back to the day when she'd accused him of having no concern for human feelings and realized how wrong she had been. She now supposed she had always known better than that, but this article was proof positive that Sam was a compassionate, feeling man. She had misjudged him horribly.

She scanned the story again, reading between the

lines to sense the sympathy Sam felt for the members of the Davis family, and Wallis was both touched and grateful that Sam had done such a thing. He didn't have to, she knew that, for he had written little for the papers lately. But this article was special, as if it were written solely for her.

Wallis pushed a strand of hair from her face and folded the paper. This was the last thing she'd expected, although she felt she should have known all along that Sam cared. He *had* cared for her, hadn't he? "I should have known," she said aloud, forgetting where she was.

"What's that?" Daphne was surprised to see Wallis's face grow pale. "Is something the matter?"

Wallis looked up, a blank expression on her face. She realized she had to say something. "Oh, it's just surprising to read something good in the paper for a change."

Fortunately the story meant little to Daphne, who brushed it aside easily, saying brightly, "Oh, political scandals are all alike—it's always another woman. Now if you don't mind, Wallis, I'm going to steal your daddy for a little while."

"Oh, no, not at all," Wallis answered, her mind on the newspaper in her hand.

"Why don't we see what there is to eat?" Daphne babbled. "I'm starving. And you can tell me all about your new horses. I understand you're raising horses now, and my oldest daughter is dying to take riding lessons."

Her father seemed to sense that Wallis was preoccupied, so he allowed himself to be led away to the bar, where a sumptuous buffet had been laid out. Wallis was grateful for once that Daphne was more interested in flirting than she was in politics, and she knew her friend would keep her father entertained. The din of the crowd had become intolerable, and she had to get away to think this new situation through. She had badly misjudged Sam, and her first instinct was somehow to make amends. Her mind was in a daze, and she had had enough of baseball for one day. Making her excuses to Ruthie Hayes, Wallis thanked her hostess for her generosity and promised to come again.

"Only if you'll pitch for us every time," Hank teased.

"You've got yourself a deal." Wallis grinned. She was determined to conceal her feelings. Blowing a kiss across the room to her parents, Wallis turned to leave. If either had been tempted to follow her, Daphne would not have allowed it. She was still talking to Judge Carmichael, who seemed completely caught up in their conversation. Rachel Carmichael raised a questioning eyebrow at her daughter but, to Wallis's great relief, just gave her a cheery wave, apparently deciding not to interfere.

A few minutes later, Wallis parked her yellow convertible in her reserved place at City Hall, her mind racing ahead to formulate a course of action. She was filled with so many conflicting emotions that, for once, she didn't know what she was going to do. She had been wrong, oh, so wrong. And she didn't know if she could ever make things right again. She had judged Sam unfairly and she didn't see how he could ever forgive her. But that didn't mean she wasn't going to ask for his forgiveness.

She had instinctively headed for the very place she worked best—her office. She knew it would be deserted this time of day—by now it was almost six o'clock—but she didn't care. This was where she did her best thinking. The sharp clicking sounds of her high-heeled pumps resounding through the empty corridors were echoes of her determination. Unlocking the door to her office, she walked in and turned on the lights. Everything had been left in good order, she noted with satisfaction. Making her way through the reception area, she entered her private office. There was only one place to start, that much was obvious. Picking up the telephone, she dialed the paper where Sam worked. She knew the city editor there, and he would know where Sam lived, or at least she hoped he would.

He has to, Wallis thought as she dialed the number. Sitting down in her chair behind the desk, she absently pulled off one earring and transferred the receiver to that ear. She glanced at her watch. Somebody has to be there, even this late, she mused, thinking back to Sam's unpredictable schedule. Somebody's down there getting out the paper, she thought, giving herself encouragement. If she had taken the time to think about what she was doing, she might not have been able to do it. But her mind was set on one objective only, and that was to find Sam.

Sure enough, the city editor was in, but Wallis's relief was short-lived. Sam had quit his job at the paper and gone back to free-lancing full time. The article she had read had been his last. No one knew where he was living, the editor said apologetically, after asking a couple of reporters who were there working late. Wallis thanked him and hung up the phone slowly, her hopes dashed.

Surely he hasn't left town without saying good-bye, she thought to herself. He wouldn't do that. He wouldn't! But even as she thought it, she knew he could have done nothing else. She had not given him an inch. Why had she been so stubborn?

Wallis got up from her desk and walked over to the window. It was dark outside, and a full moon blinked back solemnly at her from a star-filled sky. The Goodyear blimp floated by, the score of the baseball game flashing on its surface. There was no use berating herself. If she hadn't managed to get her personal life all tangled up with her professional one, her judgment might have been clearer. As it was, she had had to back away from him. She needed the distance. Too many things were going wrong. Too much needed her attention. Besides, what else could she have thought? He was a journalist and a good one, the best. It was his job to write stories. And he certainly couldn't help it if the stories were unpleasant, she realized. She shouldn't have presumed on their relationship to ask a special favor. And when he refused, she shouldn't have punished him for it. He had been right, that was all that mattered. She had been all too wrong. But now I've got to do something about all this, she told herself fiercely. I mustn't blame myself too much.

But I've certainly no one else to blame, she reminded herself bitterly. No one else at all. The thought that Sam might have left town was almost more than she could bear, and for the next several hours she threw herself into her work with all her energy. There was nothing else to do. The thought of going home again to that big, empty house was not a happy one. She would postpone that as long as she possibly could, at least until she was so tired she could count on falling asleep as soon as she went to bed.

It was nearly ten-thirty when she finished writing up a report for the budget committee. The satisfaction of having that piece of work behind her helped to dispel her downcast mood a little, but as she walked out of her office through the empty building to her car, she knew that nothing would ever completely erase the pain of losing Sam—not now, not ever.

"Good night, Your Honor," the friendly night watchman said as Wallis stepped off the elevator in the garage and headed for her car. "You sure I can't walk you to your car?" He usually made this offer on nights when she had worked late. It was obvious that he didn't like to see her out so late by herself.

"No, Chester. It's not far. I'll wave to you as I drive out. But thanks, anyway." Wallis was glad some things stayed the same, and this little bit of routine was somehow a comfort. Maybe things weren't so bad after all.

"Who are you trying to kid, Wallis Carmichael?" she said out loud to the darkness as she drove home.

One of these days you're going to have to admit to yourself that politics isn't the only passion worth having—politics isn't all there is to life, you know. You want the kind of love and desire you had with Sam. That's what's missing in your life and you know it. Political passions were all fine and good for a career, but they simply weren't enough for an entire lifetime. Wallis realized that Sam had tapped a new feeling in her—had created a need for a particular man who made her life complete. Her life might be successful without him, but it certainly wouldn't be complete.

She realized with painful clarity how much she had lost—and how foolish she had been. With a shiver of painful pleasure, she remembered her evenings with Sam—the popcorn, the movies, the joy of sharing their thoughts and the events of the day. But most of all, she remembered their lovemaking—the joyful familiarity of their bodies united in moments of sensual magic. Now that Wallis had experienced that magic, she knew she could never settle for anything less.

She had to get Sam back. She needed him in her life, now more than ever. But how—or where— would she find him? She *would* find him eventually, if she had to search high and low. Even though a mistake in judgment had lost him, she knew her determination would see it through. The short drive home passed slowly; the streets Wallis rode through saddened her because she had once shared them with Sam.

When she pulled up in front of her house, the first

thing she saw was the light in the upstairs bedroom. She hadn't left any lights on that morning—she was sure of it. But the truth was slow in coming. It wasn't until she turned into the driveway and saw Sam's motorcycle parked in the garage that her rational mind understood why her pulse had quickened. Sam! Sam was back!

Still, she got out of her car with deliberate caution. Maybe she was dreaming. She didn't dare let herself hope too much. Not yet. It might be a dream. It might go away. Shutting the car door behind her, Wallis walked over to the motorcycle and ran her hands lovingly across the handle bars. The cold metal was real enough. She was not dreaming.

"It *is* Sam," she said softly, surprised at the courage the sound of her own voice gave her. "It really is." This time she didn't shut the garage door. This time she didn't walk—she ran, until her hand found the door knob and she pushed open the front door to be greeted by the familiar smell of popcorn and butter, exactly as she knew she would. She stood at the door for a split second—long enough to catch her breath, long enough to hear the sound of popcorn popping. But that was all she needed, a split second.

"Sam," she called. "I'm home." It wasn't until she reached the kitchen door that she slowed down. But if she expected her good sense to get its bearings, it was too late. Wallis was clearly following her heart.

"Sam," she repeated breathlessly. "Hello." She stood at the door, suddenly not knowing what to say.

"What took you so long?" he asked, but his voice

was asking still another question. "I've been here for hours. I was beginning to think you might not be coming home at all."

Wallis laughed, so caught up in her joy that she didn't know where to begin. "If I'd known you were here, I'd have been home hours ago," she said happily. "I've spent a good bit of time today thinking about you and trying to find you."

She couldn't contain herself any longer and rushed into the circle of his welcoming arms. "Oh, Sam," Wallis half-sobbed, half-laughed. "Don't ever leave me again." She melted in his arms, her heart soaring as she gave herself up to the happiness she felt at being right where she belonged. "I was so afraid you didn't love me, that you were only trying to get a good story."

"You're the story I'll never write, surely you know that by now," he said, his hand holding her head against his chest. "Will you marry me, Wally? Tomorrow?"

Wallis pulled away from the welcoming circle of Sam's arms. She looked at him for a long moment, searching the expression on his face, wanting to be sure of him before she gave the only answer she wanted to give. As if she hadn't heard his question, she said shyly, "I saw your story in this afternoon's paper."

"You did?" Sam's voice was level, his blue eyes looking at her with understanding. "It's the best story I've managed to write about the whole business. By best, I mean nicest—in a human sort of way. After all, I was the one who exposed Graham. I never meant his family to suffer so terribly, and I had to do what I could to make up for it. You were my inspiration, of course, never letting up on me. That's one of the hard things about being a journalist—knowing what's important and when it's important."

He paused and then continued, "I hoped you'd read it, and when I stopped by the paper to say hello tonight, they told me you'd called. So I took the liberty of coming home." His face clouded with momentary anxiety. "It is all right, isn't it, Wally? You haven't found somebody else, have you?" His eyes searched hers, looking for an answer.

Wallis laughed. "When would I have time?" She reached over to stroke him tenderly, but when he moved toward her, she held back. "But what are you going to do? When I called the paper this afternoon, they said you'd quit."

"Right," Sam rushed on, eager to be done with the subject. "I've been free-lancing for the past several weeks, though I did the story about Davis for the paper. It was my swan song in the reporting game. You did say, after all, that a reporter and a politician couldn't have a lasting relationship. What do you think about the prospect of marrying a novelist?"

"A novelist? Oh, Sam, is it really going that well?" Her eyes shone with excitement and pride. "But what does that mean?"

"It means that I sold it!" Sam looked like the cat that swallowed the canary. "I sold my novel."

"You sold it! That's wonderful. Why didn't you tell me sooner?"

"That's exactly what I've been trying to do," Sam said indignantly. "I've been waiting for hours—"

"Okay, I get the picture," Wallis said, laughing. She leaned forward to kiss him. "It won't happen again, I promise you." She took his hand and led him upstairs.

"Does that mean you're going to marry me tomorrow?" He asked when they were standing next to the bed. He reached for her; his hands slipped her white linen jacket off and tossed it aside, then reached for the apricot silk bow tie, using the loose ends to pull her face close to his. "What do you say, Wallis Carmichael?" His lips grazed her cheek, moving quickly toward her delicate ear. Wallis tingled all over as his tongue traced the sensitive curve. His fingers busied themselves with the silk-covered buttons of her blouse, unfastening them with haste. A single finger teased the voluptuous curve of her breast and she knew she was lost, lost again to the world of sensations that only Sam could arouse in her. Wallis held her breath, realizing how much she had longed for this simple truth, the touch of his flesh against hers.

Her senses reeling under the sensual onslaught, Wallis couldn't wait any longer. "Not tomorrow, Sam," she sighed, half teasing. She quivered at his touch, tormented in a single instant by remembered delights and the promise of future pleasures.

By now Sam had removed the rest of her clothing and had pulled her down to lie full length beside him, their naked bodies touching gently, side by side.

"No?" he repeated, a look of disbelief on his face. This was not what he had expected.

"How about week after next?" Wallis asked with a grin. "In the Rose Garden at Hermann Park. I can see it now—the Goodyear blimp overhead, pulling a pair of giant lovebirds across the sky."

Sam's face broke into a tender smile, his hand reaching out to trace the features of her face with a feather touch, as if memorizing those features so dear to him. The kiss, when it came, was all the homecoming they'd expected and more. Their lips met with a tenderness that deepened into ferocious need, and their tongues joined in a sweet and salty mingling—thrusting, exploring.

After a brief moment of silence, they both began to speak at once.

"I've missed you so—"

"It's been so long—"

It really didn't matter who said what. They were together again, that was all that counted. They lay entwined in each other's arms.

Sam brushed a lock of damp hair off Wallis's forehead, his blue eyes looking into the amber depths of hers. His tender smile was quickly replaced by a wicked grin. "Well, what do we do now?" he asked, reaching down to cover her face—lips, eyelids, chin—with butterfly kisses. "Shall I read to you from my novel?" His lips moved lower to tease her neck. "Shall I make us some more popcorn?" His strong hand cupped her breast in a gesture of possessiveness. "Want to watch a movie?"

Wallis gave him a slow, provocative smile as she appeared to consider his suggestions seriously. "I think not," she said finally, her fingers reaching to caress his face. "Play it again, Sam," she started to say.

But she never got the chance.

YOU'LL BE SWEPT AWAY WITH SILHOUETTE DESIRE

$1.75 each

1 ☐ James	5 ☐ Baker	8 ☐ Dee
2 ☐ Monet	6 ☐ Mallory	9 ☐ Simms
3 ☐ Clay	7 ☐ St. Claire	10 ☐ Smith
4 ☐ Carey		

$1.95 each

11 ☐ James	29 ☐ Michelle	47 ☐ Michelle	65 ☐ Allison
12 ☐ Palmer	30 ☐ Lind	48 ☐ Powers	66 ☐ Langtry
13 ☐ Wallace	31 ☐ James	49 ☐ James	67 ☐ James
14 ☐ Valley	32 ☐ Clay	50 ☐ Palmer	68 ☐ Browning
15 ☐ Vernon	33 ☐ Powers	51 ☐ Lind	69 ☐ Carey
16 ☐ Major	34 ☐ Milan	52 ☐ Morgan	70 ☐ Victor
17 ☐ Simms	35 ☐ Major	53 ☐ Joyce	71 ☐ Joyce
18 ☐ Ross	36 ☐ Summers	54 ☐ Fulford	72 ☐ Hart
19 ☐ James	37 ☐ James	55 ☐ James	73 ☐ St. Clair
20 ☐ Allison	38 ☐ Douglass	56 ☐ Douglass	74 ☐ Douglass
21 ☐ Baker	39 ☐ Monet	57 ☐ Michelle	75 ☐ McKenna
22 ☐ Durant	40 ☐ Mallory	58 ☐ Mallory	76 ☐ Michelle
23 ☐ Sunshine	41 ☐ St. Claire	59 ☐ Powers	77 ☐ Lowell
24 ☐ Baxter	42 ☐ Stewart	60 ☐ Dennis	78 ☐ Barber
25 ☐ James	43 ☐ Simms	61 ☐ Simms	79 ☐ Simms
26 ☐ Palmer	44 ☐ West	62 ☐ Monet	80 ☐ Palmer
27 ☐ Conrad	45 ☐ Clay	63 ☐ Dee	81 ☐ Kennedy
28 ☐ Lovan	46 ☐ Chance	64 ☐ Milan	82 ☐ Clay

YOU'LL BE SWEPT AWAY WITH SILHOUETTE DESIRE

$1.95 each

83 ☐ Chance	96 ☐ Milan	109 ☐ Simms	122 ☐ Trent
84 ☐ Powers	97 ☐ James	110 ☐ Palmer	123 ☐ Paige
85 ☐ James	98 ☐ Joyce	111 ☐ Browning	124 ☐ St. George
86 ☐ Malek	99 ☐ Major	112 ☐ Nicole	125 ☐ Caimi
87 ☐ Michelle	100 ☐ Howard	113 ☐ Cresswell	126 ☐ Carey
88 ☐ Trevor	101 ☐ Morgan	114 ☐ Ross	127 ☐ James
89 ☐ Ross	102 ☐ Palmer	115 ☐ James	128 ☐ Michelle
90 ☐ Roszel	103 ☐ James	116 ☐ Joyce	129 ☐ Bishop
91 ☐ Browning	104 ☐ Chase	117 ☐ Powers	130 ☐ Blair
92 ☐ Carey	105 ☐ Blair	118 ☐ Milan	131 ☐ Larson
93 ☐ Berk	106 ☐ Michelle	119 ☐ John	132 ☐ McCoy
94 ☐ Robbins	107 ☐ Chance	120 ☐ Clay	
95 ☐ Summers	108 ☐ Gladstone	121 ☐ Browning	

SILHOUETTE DESIRE, Department SD/6
1230 Avenue of the Americas
New York, NY 10020

Please send me the books I have checked above. I am enclosing $_____
(please add 75¢ to cover postage and handling. NYS and NYC residents please
add appropriate sales tax). Send check or money order—no cash or C.O.D.'s
please. Allow six weeks for delivery.

NAME_____

ADDRESS_____

CITY_____STATE/ZIP_____

Enjoy romance and passion, larger-than-life...

Now, thrill to 4 Silhouette Intimate Moments novels (a $9.00 value) — ABSOLUTELY FREE!

If you want more passionate sensual romance, then Silhouette Intimate Moments novels are for you!

In every 256-page book, you'll find romance that's electrifying...involving... and intense. And now, these larger-than-life romances can come into your home every month!

4 FREE books as your introduction.

Act now and we'll send you four thrilling Silhouette Intimate Moments novels. They're our gift to introduce you to our convenient home subscription service. Every month, we'll send you four new Silhouette Intimate Moments books. Look them over for 15 days. If you keep them, pay just $9.00 for all four. Or return them at no charge.

We'll mail your books to you *as soon as they are published.* Plus, with every shipment, you'll receive the Silhouette Books Newsletter absolutely free. *And Silhouette Intimate Moments is delivered free.*

Mail the coupon today and start receiving Silhouette Intimate Moments. Romance novels for women...not girls.

Silhouette Intimate Moments™
120 Brighton Road, P.O. Box 5020, Clifton, NJ 07015

☐ **YES!** Please send me FREE and without obligation, 4 exciting Silhouette Intimate Moments romance novels. Unless you hear from me after I receive my 4 FREE books, please send 4 new Silhouette Intimate Moments novels to preview each month. I understand that you will bill me $2.25 each for a total of $9.00 — with no additional shipping, handling or other charges. **There is no minimum number of books to buy and I may cancel anytime I wish.** The first 4 books are mine to keep, even if I never take a single additional book.

☐ Mrs. ☐ Miss ☐ Ms. ☐ Mr.   **BMD424**

Name _____ (please print)

Address _____ Apt. #

City _____ State _____ Zip

( )
Area Code   Telephone Number

Signature (if under 18, parent or guardian must sign)

This offer, limited to one per household, expires October 31, 1984. Terms and prices are subject to change. Your enrollment is subject to acceptance by Simon & Schuster Enterprises.

Silhouette Intimate Moments is a service mark and trademark of Simon & Schuster, Inc.

Silhouette Desire

Coming Next Month

Love And Old Lace by Nicole Monet

Burned once, Virginia had decided to swear off romance and settle for a sensible, chaste existence—but seductive Lucas Freeman stormed her defenses and neither her body nor her heart could resist.

Wilderness Passion by Lindsay McKenna

Libby wanted to be ready for anything when she met her unwilling partner on the environmental expedition. But nothing prepared her for Dan Wagner, and the mountain trek suddenly became a journey into a world of desire.

Table For Two by Josephine Charlton

Hadley and Lucas had shared a youthful love. Now, when Hadley had landed in his embrace once more, history repeated itself and left them both determined that this time they would not have to say goodbye.

The Fires Within by Aimee Martel

As a female firefighter, Isabel was determined to be "one of the boys"—but no one made her feel more a woman than Lt. Mark Grady. Passion blazed between them, but could they be lovers *and* co-workers?

Tide's End by Erin Ross

Chemical engineer on an offshore oil rig, Holly had vowed never to engage in a "platform romance." Kirk's touch could make her forget her promises, but would his dangerous job as a diver keep them apart?

Lady Be Bad by Elaine Raco Chase

Though Noah had broken her heart six years before, Marlayna still loved him. Now she would attend his wedding with only one aim in mind—she would break all the rules to have him back again.